SEDUCTION Games

ALLYSON LINDT

Copyright © 2017 by Allyson Lindt
All Rights Reserved

ISBN: 978-1543196856

Manufactured in the United States of America
Acelette Press

Other Books in this Series

Control Games (Game for Cookies Book 2)

For my eternal dragon

Table of Contents

Chapter One

I heard the screaming as I slid the key into the lock, but it didn't penetrate my haze of bummed-out enough to make sense. I pushed open the door to the apartment I shared with my boyfriend, and my eyes confirmed what my brain hadn't quite registered. James, half-kneeling on the couch, pants around his ankles, screwing a woman I'd never seen before.

Time ground to a stop long enough for nausea to surge in my gut and burn my throat.

"That's *her?*" The disdain in the other woman's voice heated my cheeks to scalding.

James scrambled to extract himself from the compromising position.

I clenched my jaw, not sure if I wanted to scream or cry. Neither. Fuck this. I turned away from the sight without a single word, and strode into the kitchen. The champagne in the fridge was to celebrate me finally getting the loan I needed, to expand my business.

Well, that hadn't happened. And apparently, my boyfriend not cheating on me was also out of the question. I spun back toward the front door. I wouldn't scream. Or cry. Or give these people any satisfaction. I could lose my shit once I got to my car.

"Andrea, wait." James stepped in my path, fumbling to button his jeans.

I hated it when he called me that. My growl, combined with my expression, must have been enough to convey what I couldn't find the words for, because he stepped aside.

"Andi, please?"

"Now you get it right?" Six months together, and I could count on one hand them number of times he'd called me by my preferred name. Maybe that should have been a sign. I didn't look back, as I slammed the door behind me—with any luck catching his finger or his dick in the process—and stormed back to my car.

My mind was numb, as I pulled back into rush-hour traffic. The only thought I could focus on was, *why don't I feel anything?*

About ten minutes into my drive, it hit me. A giant, suffocating wave that knocked aside disbelief and sent tears spilling down my cheeks. I struggled to find my breath and keep focused long enough to pull off the road. I found a spot in the back of a grocery store parking lot, and sobbed until my eyes ached and my hiccups for air made my stomach hurt.

Fucking asshole had cheated on me. Was it a one-time thing, or had this been going on for a while? Since before I moved in, a few months ago? Or right about the time he started telling me work had him so stressed out, he wasn't interested in sex?

Not that it mattered. We were over. Nothing he could say would make up for this.

Someone knocked on my car window. A guy in a red shirt with the store logo. "Are you okay?" His question filtered through the glass.

I dragged my hand across my cheeks, smearing the tears more than wiping them away, and nodded.

"You sure?"

I nodded again and forced myself to give him a smile. I must look horrible. Puffy red eyes. Runny nose. I didn't care. I did want to get out of here before anyone else stumbled on me, which meant finding a place to go. My best friend, Julie, was out of town, scouting new locations for our cookie business. I'd insisted we needed the money first, and I wasn't leaving town for it. I guess the second part didn't matter anymore, but we still didn't have the money. Motel it was. I'd only be there for the night, anyway. That was, if the trip was still on.

A new wave of suffocating sadness, hurt, and rage blanketed me.

Fuck it. Of course it was. James was only going to keep me company. I'd go without the asshole. Give me some time away, to clear my head. I navigated to the closest motel, checked in, and moments later collapsed on my bed, champagne bottle clutched in my hand.

I'd walked out of the apartment without any of my stuff. My bags for tomorrow's trip sat near the bedroom door. My clothes hung in the closet, and my toiletries were in the bathroom. Maybe I should have thought this through. Or not. I couldn't have stuck around longer. My mind wouldn't have been able to handle it. At least I had my laptop with me. I'd need that for the trip. We were—correction, I was—driving from Omaha to Las Vegas, for a national gaming competition. The plan was to meet the other two guys from my team there. We didn't have any illusions of winning, but since we'd been good enough to qualify, and all had some vacation time, we decided what the hell? Road trip.

It was also supposed to be a romantic getaway with James. Maybe help him get over the stress of work. See if we could find that spark a new couple in their late twenties shouldn't have to worry about missing in the first place. So much for that idea.

My palm started to ache, and I rolled my head sideways. My fingers were stiff from still clenching the bottle neck of the champagne. Then there was this failure. The bubbly set aside to celebrate a victory I hadn't achieved—finding the funding I needed to expand my cookie business and finally make it a full time venture, so I could stop processing insurance claims to pay the bills.

A new layer of sadness drifted in, and I swept it aside. I refused to wallow. I had expensive booze, a hotel room to myself, and Wi-Fi. I was going to enjoy it.

I kicked out of my shoes, toed off my socks, and went in search of something to drink from. My quest was rewarded when I found plastic cups on the sink counter. I sat cross-legged on my bed, laptop open in front of me, and bubbly in hand.

Two hours later, I had more champagne in me than remained in the bottle, and a warm, fluffy cloud of *I don't give a fuck* floated through my head. James could rot in Hell, for all I cared. Our relationship had been falling apart anyway. I saw that now.

I still needed clothes for my trip. I licked my lips, then grimaced. And toothpaste. Or maybe I'd go naked. I giggled at the thought. Go find a guy, to prove to James I didn't need him.

My messenger chimed with two notifications. Isaiah and Kane had logged on. A grin threatened to split my face, and I sent them a joint message.

Are you in town?

They were my gaming partners, but they lived in Chicago. They were part of the grand road-trip plan. They'd stop here for the night, meet us for breakfast in the morning, and we'd follow each other the rest of the way west.

We are. Isaiah responded first. *If you're online, does that mean you're done celebrating?*

I laughed at the empty room, and sent back a *LOLOLOLOLOLOL. The only thing I'm celebrating is bashe…* I backspaced. *Bachalar…* I deleted it again. *Singleness, and how good booze makes my head feel.*

Geez, Andi. That was Kane. *Are you all right? What's going on?*

I'm fine. They must both be in their hotel room, probably cuddled up together in bed. At least,

5

that was the way I pictured them. The perfect guys. The sweetest, most adorable couple. *I'm all warm and fuzzy.* My stomach lurched. *I think I forgot to eat.*

What's going on? Kane asked again.

It took me several tries, punctuated with flipping off my keyboard for being an asshole, but I managed to relate my day.

So sorry, Isaiah offered.

James was a dick anyway, Kane added.

I wasn't sure which sentiment I appreciated more. *I don't want to talk about it. How was your drive? Are the two of you all cuddly and naked and waiting for me to stop talking, so you can get it on?*

The drive was good, Isaiah said. *You need sleep.*

I scowled at the way he'd ignored my second question. A tiny voice in the back of my head told me I wasn't thinking straight. What did it know? *I'll sleep later. I'm alone in a motel room, in nothing but a T-shirt and panties, and I want some sexy details to keep me company. I'll share in return.*

Even though I'd never met them face to face, I'd known Isaiah and Kane far longer than James. Long enough to know they had an open relationship and were fluid in their preferences. Sometimes they picked up a girl together. On more than one occasion—before James anyway—our late night conversations started with me getting descriptions of how exactly that worked, and ended with some amazing, graphic cybersex between the three of us. Stories about *her* became details of the things they'd do to me. Fuzzy images floated through my head

6

now, teasing and wanting Kane and Isaiah to fill in the blanks.

Sleep, Andi, Kane said. *We'll see you in the morning.*

Pout I want help putting me to sleep.

Not while you're drunk, Andi... I could almost hear the warning in Isaiah's words.

Fine. I scowled at the empty room, which danced around me in return, sparkly and bright. He was looking out for me, not angry, but the rejection still stung. *One more favor, though?*

Depends. I'd spent enough time listening to Kane over the headphones, I assumed his words were clipped at this point.

I hadn't meant to piss him off. *Can I drive with you guys this trip? My car's not going to make it.*

Of course, Kane replied. *Do you still want to meet us at the same place?*

There's a coffee shop by my motel. If that's okay. I'll send the address.

We'll be there. Get some sleep.

At least they were concerned about me. We said our goodnights, and I shut everything off. Sleep wasn't my friend, though. The room swam again when I lay down, and I spent the next hour hunched over the toilet, heaving and hating the way champagne tasted coming back up. When I finally drifted off to sleep, my dreams weren't any kinder. Images of James fucking that woman, and her, *That's her?* danced through my dreams all night.

7

Chapter Two

I didn't care that I wore my sunglasses inside a Kmart. Those fluorescents were bright. My skull protested every time I turned my head too quickly. I was meeting the guys in half an hour, and I could barely think enough to grab some jeans, T-shirts, and other basic necessities, so I wouldn't be naked in Las Vegas.

My head pounded harder at the word *naked*. God, I'd made a fool of myself last night. Had I really said those things to them? Remorse and my spinning gut told me yes.

I was paying for my purchases, when my phone buzzed against my hip. I squinted, to read the text message from Julie. *Were you drunk FB-ing last night?*

Was I? Crap. *Probably.*

Seconds later, my ringtone clawed its way

into my eardrums. I grabbed my stuff from the cashier, gave him a weak smile, and walked toward the exit before answering. "Yeah."

"Talk to me. Did he really cheat on you?" Julie's sympathetic tone hammered my thoughts.

"Did I say that?"

"Not in so many words." She clucked. "What you did was change your relationship status to *Looking for someone who understands what mutually exclusive means*."

That sounded like me. "Did I at least spell exclusive right?"

"Yup. Are you okay?"

"I'm fine. I mean, no, but it hasn't killed me yet." I had enough time to get back to my motel, take the fastest shower in history, and scrub this layer of gross out of my mouth with my new toothbrush, before meeting the guys. I dropped into my car and took a second to luxuriate in the wonder of sitting.

"I'll be back tomorrow. We'll commiserate together. Whatever you want to do," Julie said.

"I can't. Vegas, remember?"

"You're going anyway? Not with *him*, right?"

I was glad she didn't say his name. Just the thought of James made me want to puke. "Hell, no. Isaiah and Kane."

"What?" Julie's tone shifted to a high-pitched, drill-into-my-thoughts pitch that would have cost me my breakfast if I'd eaten any. She didn't think internet people were real.

"Picking me up is on their way, and they're already in town." I didn't know why I was making excuses. I didn't have a problem with them.

"I know they're your gaming partners, but you don't know them, and there's a lot of nowhere between here and Las Vegas."

I really needed to get going. And also, to not let her talk me out of this. Doubt was already asking if she had a good point. "Given the events of the last twenty-four or so hours, I don't have a lot of respect for gut feelings right now. Look, I need to go." I cut her off before she could toss out more logic I might feel compelled to agree with, if I thought about it too long. "I'll text you when we stop for the night. I promise."

"Andi…"

"Laters." My voice had too much cheer in it, as I hung up.

A short while later, I stepped into the coffee shop with a couple minutes to spare. The shower erased some of my hangover. Brushing my teeth helped more. I ordered the biggest drink I could get, with as many shots of espresso as were legal. The first few sips tasted funny, mixed with mint, but it was better than what had been growing on my tongue half an hour ago. I set myself up to see the parking lot, and tried to relax.

A green Explorer with Illinois plates pulled into an empty spot, and a new kind of nervous tension spilled into me. It was a silly response. I'd known these guys for more than two years. We had each other's backs online, and our friendship was solid. Julie didn't get that. Or maybe my stress came from the way I'd acted last night. They'd forgive me, right?

My thoughts trailed off when they climbed from the SUV. Okay, they weren't supposed to be gorgeous. They were attractive enough in their photos, but real life always told a different story. Kane had been driving, and I got a good look at his long legs, wiry frame, and every inch of defined chest under his fitted T-shirt when he unfolded himself from his seat. His blond hair flopped into his eyes, and he raked it back.

Isaiah was his opposite in everything but height. Both almost reached the top of the car roof. But Isaiah's jet black hair was cut short, and sunglasses covered his eyes. His long-sleeved shirt didn't hide how broad his shoulders were, or the solid muscle underneath his clothes.

I tugged at my sloppy, still-wet ponytail. Maybe I should have put on some makeup. I had mascara and lip gloss in my purse. Too late now. They made it inside and walked toward me. I shifted my weight from one foot to the other, and gave them my best smile. How was one supposed to initiate a greeting like this?

"Andi?" Isaiah asked. With his sunglasses off, it was obvious how pale, clear, and gorgeous blue his eyes were. The stark contrast with his hair almost stole my breath.

I nodded.

He wrapped me in a huge hug. "I'm glad we get to meet you, finally."

"Me too." I squeezed back, and when he let me go, I turned to Kane. "Hey."

His hug was more tentative. Still warm and friendly, but almost as if he thought he had to. Or

11

maybe he was upset about last night. The memory rushed back, hazy but just as embarrassing.

"I'm sorry about what I said on chat."

"No worries." Kane bent at the waist and grabbed my duffel bag. "Are you doing better now?"

"I'm not wasted anymore. *Better* is a relative term."

"Of course." Isaiah squeezed my fingers. "Is that all you have?"

"I kind of walked out without grabbing anything." My laptop and purse hung from my shoulder. It was tough to let those leave my side. I'd have to go back to James's for my stuff eventually. It would wait, though. At least this conversation was comfortable. Any anxiety I had about meeting them in person evaporated.

"I'm going to grab us breakfast." Isaiah gestured toward the counter. "You two get loaded into the Explorer. Do you have everything you need?"

"Coffee. Clothes. Knights in shining armor. I'm good." My smile felt genuine for the first time since yesterday. The gnawing hurt and frustration of James cheating on me hovered at the back of my mind, but it was easy enough to ignore if I focused on everything else.

Like the fact Kane smelled amazing—woodsy and clean—when he rested a palm on my lower back and pointed me toward the car. "You should hook up, once we get there." Teasing filled his voice. "Get that dick out of your system."

I adored that this was his version of trying to

cheer me up. Especially since it echoed what I'd been thinking last night. Of course, it was a drunk, vindictive idea I'd never follow through on, but it was fun to joke about. "Maybe. Maybe I'll find a guy, or even two, to prove how much better off I am."

He set my bag in the back and cradled my laptop it in a more secure section, before turning back to me. He studied my face for a moment, expression unreadable. "Exactly."

We hit the road a few minutes later. Their drive from Chicago yesterday had only been about eight hours, and today would be the longest leg of the trip. The hope was to hit Utah before we were too tired to continue for the night. If we swapped out drivers, it wouldn't be an issue. We could drive straight through, with all three of us here, but the competition didn't start for three more days, so there was no reason to exhaust ourselves before we got there.

The banter flowed more easily than I expected, and I found myself sinking into the casual conversation. It was just like being online, but now I could see the way they moved their hands when they spoke and hear the inflections in their voices that the microphone muffled. I leaned back against the seat and closed my eyes, letting the July sun warm my face and chase away the last of my hangover.

"Andi." Someone shook my shoulder, and Isaiah's voice burrowed into my thoughts. "Wake up, Dee."

I pried open my eyes, and shut them again when the sun hit them. My neck ached, and so did my throat. I pushed myself upright and braved looking again.

Isaiah sat next to me, brows furrowed in concern. He traced a thumb across my cheek. "Are you sure you're okay?"

"Of course." The words came out raspier than I intended. "Why?"

"You fell asleep while we were talking."

"Oh, crap. I'm so sorry." They were going to think I was a social moron if I kept doing things like drunkenly throwing myself at them and passing out during conversations.

"It's okay. I have a feeling you didn't sleep much last night. But we stopped, to give me an excuse to check on you."

Geez. I rubbed my face. I'd been dreaming about… I wasn't sure. "I'm okay." The last thing I wanted was him staring at half-asleep, bleary-eyed me. "Where are we?"

"Denver. Are you sure?"

"Of course." I forced myself to smile and not drag up whatever was shadowy and hovering at the back of my mind. "I need to wash my face, and stuff."

He nodded toward a diner connected to the gas station. "We'll be in there. Come find us."

"Be there soon." I climbed from the SUV and made my way toward the restroom sign. Grief nudged the back of my thoughts, and I pushed it aside. It was a fucked up dream, combined with hangover residue. Nothing more. And once I got some food in my stomach, it would stop protesting and telling me otherwise.

Chapter Three

About five hours later, we pulled into Grand Junction, Colorado. It wasn't quite Utah, but it was close, and we'd make Las Vegas in plenty of time tomorrow. Whatever plagued my dreams earlier—being pissed off at James; I was sure of it—had passed. The rest of the drive had been friendly and fun, and I managed to stay awake the entire time.

We stopped at the first diner we found, and I excused myself to go freshen up. When I saw my reflection in the restroom mirror, I couldn't help but make faces. My ponytail hadn't done anything to tame my mane of curls, once my hair dried, and a large puff of brown frizz extruded from the back of my skull. I grabbed my brush and two hair elastics, and did something I hadn't in ages—pulled the high-frizz mess into two braids, one on each side of my head. It wasn't long enough for much else. I looked young this way, almost childish, but it would keep it out of my face.

I found Isaiah and Kane already settled in a booth in the back of the restaurant. Isaiah talked with his hands, gesturing wildly, while Kane mostly nodded. The adoration in their eyes when they looked at each other made my footsteps falter. I resumed walking, unable to shake a single thought. What would it be like to have someone to look at that way, who returned the feeling? James and I never had that. The realization struck me hard and left a hollow ache in my chest.

I swallowed it all and slid into the booth seat across from them.

"Welcome back." Kane grinned.

"Perfect." Isaiah turned to me. "He was telling the brilliant idea the two of you came up with."

Even though they both looked completely relaxed, something about his words set me on edge. "Which was…?"

"You need to get laid."

Kane rolled his eyes. "I didn't put it quite that way."

I dropped my face into my hands, heat flushing my cheeks at the direct suggestion. It carried a hint of imagery with it, built on some of the conversations we'd shared in the past. Kane's mouth on mine. Isaiah's hands roaming my body. Desire flooded my skin. That probably wasn't what they meant. "How did you put it?" I asked.

"I think the term I used was *revenge fuck*."

That wasn't any better. Fantasy rolled in, painting mental pictures of one of them pinning me down, cock sliding inside me, while the other sucked and pinched my nipples. I reached for my ice water and took a long swallow. "Still not following you."

"We need to find you a guy at the competition." Isaiah leaned in and rested his forearms on the edge of the table. He locked his gaze on me. "Someone gorgeous, smart, or at least who knows when not to talk, who understands this is only for one night. To help you move on."

The idea sounded as fantastic and as completely unrealistic as the last two times it came up. "I don't know how to pick up guys. What am I supposed to do? Walk up to people I find attractive and say, *Hey, wanna help me get over my cheating jerk of an ex-boyfriend by screwing my brains out?*"

They exchanged glances before looking back at me. Kane shrugged. "Why not?"

"Because I'm plain, boring, terminally shy little me."

"Says the woman who asked us for details about our sex life last night." There was no irritation in Kane's voice.

"I was drunk. And I said I was sorry."

"And it's not an issue." Isaiah reached across the table and covered my hand with his. "You're not plain at all. Or boring. You look gorgeous right now. And you're going to be the confident woman at a competition filled with gamer guys. You'll have your pick."

The compliment warmed me from the inside out. It didn't stop me from noticing another flaw in his plan. "I don't want most of those guys. Even for a night."

"You're not looking for your soul mate," Kane said. "You want someone attractive to fuck the hell out of you, so you have bragging rights when you go back home."

"I can't do that."

"Why not?" Isaiah asked.

"Because... You really want a list? It's a long freaking list."

Kane held up his index finger. "Name one thing."

I had a hard enough time finding and keeping steady boyfriends. James had been number three in my entire life. I was awkward around people. There was no way I could flirt with a random stranger. Every reason died on my lips, each sounding lamer than the last. "I don't know how."

Kane nudged Isaiah, and they shared another look. That would be nice—to have conversations without ever saying a word. Isaiah squeezed my hand before pulling away. "We'll teach you."

"How to seduce a guy?" I couldn't keep the disbelief from my voice. "I don't think that's a *teachable* kind of thing. Especially in the next two days."

Kane raised his brows and drew his lips into a thin line. "If you're not interested, say *no*."

I was, though. As completely implausible as the outcome seemed, I liked the idea of feeding James a taste of his own medicine, and I couldn't have asked for more gorgeous or patient instructors. "I'm interested. When do we start?"

"Now." Isaiah scooted to my side of the booth, boxing me in. His heat seeped into my arm, drawing already tingling nerve endings further to life. He shifted so he faced me, knee resting on the vinyl and pressing into my leg. When he tugged on one of my braids, I almost groaned. Where had that come from?

When I got a room tonight and had a little alone time, I was going to spend some time gliding my fingers over every inch of my body where these two touched in my fantasies. It was kind of a shame I'd left my vibrator behind, but over the past few months, I'd gotten good at getting myself off while James snored away next to me. At least tonight, I wouldn't have to be quiet.

"First things first." Isaiah rested his hand on my shoulder. "Relax."

"I— What?"

He kneaded the muscle, and this time I did groan. I didn't realize I was that wound up.

"You're thinking about it too hard." His voice was low and soothing. "Just be yourself."

"What if mister tall-dark-and-for-one-night-only doesn't like me as myself?"

"Then find someone worth your time," Kane said.

"You make it sound easy."

Isaiah leaned in, breath caressing my skin, and whispered, "It is." He never made contact, but if I shifted my head a little to the right, his lips would brush my ear. "Any guy worth anything would fall to his knees and beg for a night with you, if he thought it would work. We're going to prove it to you."

I pulled away enough to look him in the eye. His gaze almost sank into my soul, and sincerity stared back. He gave me a tiny smile. "I promise." His voice was smooth and confident.

I had no illusions it was that simple, but I was going to let myself fall into pretending at least a little longer if it meant this kind of up-close-and-personal attention.

Chapter Four

"So, what else?" I wanted more solid advice, but a tiny voice in the back of my head reminded me it had only been a day since the James incident. I argued back that was why we were doing this.

"Nothing else. Approach. Make small talk. Ask him out." Kane made it sound as straightforward as a convenience-store run for more Dew.

"I suck at small talk. There are only so many times I'll want to hear how hot it is. It's Las Vegas in July. It's going to be hotter than the underside of Satan's balls."

Someone coughed, and I realized a waitress stood next to our table. "You need another minute?" Her tone was flat, but the corners of her mouth twitched as if she was struggling not to laugh.

Isaiah squeezed my knee and turned in his seat. "Nah, we're ready."

I started to protest, but as Isaiah ordered, Kane slid the menu to me, finger resting on a turkey avocado sandwich. Apparently I was predictable, even to two people I'd only just met in person. Why didn't James ever figure me out the way they had? I shook the thought aside before it became misery.

The waitress made notes and left. Isaiah turned back to me. "You do fine with us."

"Small talk." Kane added. "Or rather, we never run out of things to talk about."

"That's different. I know you. If I say, *Do you ever wonder why we're here* — *?*"

"That's one of life's great mysteries, isn't it? Why *are* we here?" Kane didn't miss a beat, coming in with the opening line from *Red vs. Blue.*

I couldn't help my grin. "See?"

"Use that as an opener for every guy you approach." Isaiah leaned back when the waitress returned with our drinks, so she could set mine in front of me. "If he follows it up right, you know he's worth at least a fraction of your time."

"But that's our thing." Maybe I was being silly, but the fact we slid into the obscure reference without pause felt special.

"Technically, it's Rooster Teeth's thing," Isaiah swirled his straw in his drink, clinking the ice.

Kane leaned back to rest against the wall instead of the bench. "Do we have to pay them every time we say that?"

As flattering as the attention had been, this was much better than them trying to coach me. "We just need to give proper attribution. Right?"

"Unless they're litigious," Kane said.

I laughed. "Ooh, big word."

"And one I'd bet money"—he pulled his wallet out—"you can't spell, when you're drunk."

I stuck my tongue out at him. "I don't have to. I'm not the one who's lawsuit happy."

We slid from one topic to the next, as we finished our food, nursed our drinks, and pretended the hours weren't vanishing. As the clock on the diner wall reached ten, I had to admit we might need to call it a night. "We need to get rooms. If they have any left, that is."

"Rooms? Plural?" Isaiah asked.

"It's the middle of nowhere. They have a room left." Kane slid from his seat anyway, and held a hand out for Isaiah. "If you get your own, it's going to cost extra, and we have to say goodbye until tomorrow morning. You know the Wi-Fi here is gonna suck."

"We'll get a double queen." Isaiah helped me stand. "Just one room."

"If you're sure…" I didn't actually have any desire to protest. I was having too much fun to say goodnight, but it felt like the polite thing to do.

Isaiah wrapped an arm around my waist, and a rush of giddiness filled me. This was nice. He hooked his thumb into my belt loop and twisted me toward the walkway joining the diner to the motel. "Come on, roomie."

Moments later, we were settled in one room. I sat on my mattress with my legs crossed. Kane mirrored my posture, with Isaiah behind him, arm draped over Kane's shoulder.

As a comfortable silence drifted between us,

23

a new thought plowed its way into my mind, and I scowled. Not what I wanted to worry about right now.

"Spit it out," Kane said.

It didn't matter that we'd discussed almost everything in the time we knew each other, this was one secret I kept tucked away, nicely wrapped in a ball of I'd-rather-not-ever-admit-it. "Don't worry about it."

"Dee." Isaiah's tone was a combination of coaxing and warning.

I chewed my lip, indecision rocking inside me. Everything about life told me it was something to be embarrassed about, but at the same time, I didn't think they'd have a problem with it. I dredged up the confession. "The plan is I hook up with some random guy, right? What if I'm not experienced enough for him? What if we get back to his room and he's like, *Uh, wow, you're boring in bed.*"

Isaiah frowned and scooted to the edge of the bed, to dangle his legs over the side. "I don't think you have to worry about that."

Frustration and embarrassment built inside. "I'm twenty eight, and I've had three boyfriends in my life. The first was high school, and we did some really intense making out. The second made fun of me and called me gay, because I thought it was hot to watch people enjoy sex, regardless of their gender, and the third..." I trailed off, not wanting to talk about James. "Let's just say, in the end they all went somewhere else for sex."

"I've heard you in chat, Dee. You've got a wicked sexy imagination on you, whether or not it's

24

drawn from experience."

I tapped my toes against the inside of my leg. "But saying and doing are two separate things."

Kane raised his brows. "How so?"

"Really?" I couldn't believe he'd just asked that. Partly because I didn't want to have to explain. "Just because I read a book on brain surgery, and know the terminology, doesn't mean I can operate. Besides, dirty talk is different over the internet than looking someone in the eye."

Isaiah stood, pulled me to my feet, and moved behind me. "Better?" he asked.

I laughed and shook my head. "Not so much."

He trailed a finger along the back of my neck, lightly enough to send a pleasant chill down my spine. "What kind of things are you saying online that you've never done in real life?"

"Like, most of it." I wanted to close my eyes and sink into Isaiah's touch. I couldn't make eye contact with Kane, so that helped the impulse. I resisted the urge and studied my feet instead.

Kane rose and closed the distance between us. Finger under my chin, he forced my gaze to his. "Be specific."

What did he want me to say? "My sex life has been limited to lying on my back, guy thrusting between my legs until he's done, then him rolling over and passing out while I finish myself off." The words spilled out with more force than I intended, carried on the pent-up frustration of having lived the story.

"I'd like to see that sometime." Isaiah's

breath caressed my ear, chasing away the lingering traces of anger that came with the memories.

I let out a shaky breath. "My sexual frustration?"

"You finishing yourself off." He kissed the back of my neck so lightly, I almost thought I imagined it.

My breath caught, and I struggled to bring my libido under control before it got ideas of its own. "This is still about training, right?" Part of me wished I hadn't asked. Wanted to get lost in the moment and pretend it was anything but innocent banter among friends. I'd just had my heart ripped out, though. I wasn't ready for that again.

"Sure. Of course." Isaiah rested his hands on my hips. "If you're worried about being uncomfortable when you get back to random-stranger-guy's room, maybe we can ease you into looking forward to it."

I bit the inside of my cheek. This was the bit where I should tell them we needed our sleep. And I might have, if it weren't for the flames racing through my veins, and every inch of my skin pleading for a hands-on taste of being *eased into.* "What did you have in mind?"

Kane shook his head and dropped his hand. "Not us. You. What is it you're afraid of failing at? Be specific."

"Everything." I couldn't make myself form actual descriptive sentences. It really was different in real life. Over chat, I heard their voices, but there were no expressions. No actual contact. No visual cues that the moment was disappointing. Over chat, everyone enjoyed it, because it was all fantasy.

"*Everything* is vague." Kane looked me over. Everywhere his gaze fell, the desire to be touched followed. "For instance, have you ever had a guy strip you down a piece of clothing at a time, and visually drink in that gorgeous body of yours?"

My answer stuck in my throat, as images and phantom sensations accompanied his question. My nipples tightened against my bra, begging to be freed. "No," I managed.

Kane tucked a finger inside the waistband of my jeans and glided it, caressing my skin. "Would you like to?"

Chapter Five

I really, really liked the idea. My mind worked overtime with whispers of what this would lead to. I hovered at the edge of *yes,* terrified of what crossing that line meant.

Isaiah whispered, "It's all part of the learning process, Dee. No strings. No commitment. We promise."

"Yes." Saying the word sent a new wave of desire coursing through me, unfurling in my belly and pulsing between my thighs.

Kane's smile was wicked and hungry. He tugged up the bottom of my T-shirt, and then yanked it over my head. The cool air of the fan was a sharp contrast to my heated skin. I expected to be ashamed, standing between them almost topless. Instead dampness spread between my legs, at the two sets of eyes on me.

Isaiah's short nails scuffed my back as he unhooked my bra, then he dragged the straps down my arms. My nipples were already hard points, bright pink in the open air and begging to be touched. Would I get that chance? My heart hammered against my ribs in anticipation.

Kane undid my jeans and pushed them and my panties to the floor. He never made contact more than was necessary to strip off my clothes, but the way he studied me felt like a million fingers dancing over my skin. Silence descended between us until I was pretty sure my hammering pulse roared over the air conditioner. "What now?" I forced myself to ask.

Isaiah stood close enough to my back, his warmth reached me, but he didn't touch me again. "What do *you* want now?"

"This is about me being inexperienced, remember?"

"No." Kane traced the outline of my frame with his hand, but never came close enough for me to feel the caress. "This is about you learning to ask for what you want. You want the cute guy at the competition? You ask him out. Invite him up to your room." He stepped closer and hovered his palm above my breast. "If you want me to touch you, tell me where."

This entire situation was absurd. Straight out of a cheesy porn movie—not that I minded those if the actors enjoyed themselves. It wasn't the kind of thing that happened in real life, though. Two guys teaching their inexperienced friend how to have good sex, so she could hook up with someone else? Implausible.

It was also incredibly enticing, and there was no way I would turn down the chance. I licked my lips, to bring some of the moisture back into them, and tried to pull a coherent request from my scrambling brain. "I like my nipples played with."

He traced a thumb over the rigid peak, and I gasped at the thread of pleasure the motion tugged inside. "Hard or soft?" he asked.

"Hard."

He moved both hands into place, one on each side, and rolled my nipples between his fingers. With each tug or pinch, a new throb of desire spiked through my sex.

Isaiah wrapped his arms around my waist, and I groaned at the contrast in his tender touch compared to Kane's. Isaiah traced tiny circles over my hips with his thumbs. "Do you want more?"

I nodded.

"Tell him."

"I like them sucked on."

Kane lowered his mouth to one breast and flicked his tongue over the swollen nub.

"God, yes." I whimpered and thrust against his mouth. The rough texture of his tongue and the occasional bite stole the oxygen from my head.

Isaiah glided his palms lower and paused just below my waist. "What else do you like? What else would you like to try?"

I swallowed and tried to figure out what to ask for next. My pulsing clit wanted attention, and that was always where I zeroed in, when I wanted to get off. This was different. It was heady and intoxicating and consuming. The goal was the same though, right? "You could put your fingers between my legs."

Isaiah's hand crept down, while Kane continued to lavish my breasts with attention. Isaiah asked, "Do you ever use a vibrator?"

"Sometimes. But they're noisy, and I like..." The confession died in my throat.

"Like what?" He hesitated above my slit, ticking the tender skin.

"When I'm turned on, I like the tactile sensation." I'd said these things before. To them, even. With each new word, it got a little easier. "I like feeling how wet I get. Playing with my clit myself."

He dipped his fingers between my folds, and pleasure burst forward inside. He didn't linger long enough to make me come, but the new touch kept me hovering at the edge. I squirmed between them, not sure which sensation to focus on, the combined attentions holding me at the brink of climax. Isaiah traced circles around my clit, tightening them until my breathing burst out in shallow gasps. He eased off, and Kane pinched and sucked, before pulling away long enough to blow lightly across a damp nipple.

I tried to get closer to both touches, but it seemed as if each time I shifted, one of them backed away enough to deny me release.

"That can't be all you like." Isaiah kissed along my bare shoulder.

He obviously expected more input, but right now the only thing I could think of was coming against his hand. "I don't know. What do you recommend?"

He kissed the edge of my ear. "Handcuffs."

The single word sent a new shock through my frame. I didn't know if the idea of being bound terrified or enticed me, and I wasn't sure how it would get me off now.

"Maybe another night." Isaiah dipped a finger inside me, before moving back up my slit, to tease again. "That is, if you're interested another night. What else do you want right now? Unless you're worn out?"

I wasn't. But I did trip over the implication we might do this again. There was one thing I wanted that I almost always got with them online. "Both of you." I swallowed. "Inside me at the same time." I didn't think it would work, but they insisted it was possible.

Isaiah honed in on my clit, teasing the swollen button until I couldn't breathe. "I like the way you think." He stroked me until pleasure spilled through my body, stealing my desire to stand. Making my head swim. Sparking colors behind my eyes. I was pretty sure I screamed when I came, grinding into his hand until I couldn't take it anymore.

Kane moved his mouth to mine and kissed me with a hunger I'd never tasted before. It dragged out the pleasant edges of my climax and sang through my senses. He pulled back, searching my eyes. "Are you sure?"

It was actually going to happen? I would have asked for clarification, but I didn't want to destroy the moment. "Yes. But you're both wearing too many clothes."

Kane nodded at Isaiah. "You heard the lady."

I wasn't sure who to focus on, as they undressed. Both men were sexy. Kane with his thin frame and defined torso. Isaiah covered in muscle. Both with cocks standing at attention—and wow, I'd never been with someone so well-endowed before. I reached toward Kane, then hesitated. Was I allowed to do this?

He grabbed my wrist, trailed my finger down his chest, and wrapped my palm around his dick. I thought my skin was hot, but his almost burned me. He hissed when I stroked. "You need to work on that asking for what you want thing." His words filtered through clenched teeth.

Isaiah passed something over my shoulder, and I realized the little square was a condom. At least they were prepared. I tried not to put too much thought into why. I knew—or at least I assumed from the things they said in chat—they didn't use those with each other.

Kane rolled his protection on, then took my hands again. He guided me along, as he stepped back toward the bed. "This takes a little squishing and maneuvering"—he sat on the edge of the mattress, then tugged on me—"but it can be amazing." He locked his gaze on mine. "And fuck, I want to feel you riding me."

I straddled his legs and hovered above his erection. Hands on my hips, he glided inside. I was still wet, so there wasn't much friction, but he stretched me out. I sighed as I sank onto his shaft. If I wasn't as hungry for Isaiah as I was for Kane, I'd say

33

this was enough. The way he rocked inside me, tight and slow, and the clench of his jaw making me think he was holding back, amped my desire.

He slid his hands to my back and pulled me to him. He lay a series of nibbles along my lower lip before claiming my mouth and driving his tongue inside. I pressed into him, molding my body to his, wanting to be a part of him. He slid his hands to my ass, and shock pricked my senses when something cool glided along my crack. A finger, probably covered in lube.

"Relax." Isaiah's calm tone was a sharp contrast to the ravenous kiss consuming half my attention.

I drank in Kane's touch. Tangled my fingers in his hair. Dove into the pocket encompassing all three of us.

I started when something else nudged my back entrance. Kane pulled my gaze back to him. His brown eyes were wide and wild. Frightening, in a seductive, ethereal way. "Don't think about it too much." He kissed down my chin and to my throat, his words rumbling through my flesh. "Focus on how it feels, not what he's doing."

I gasped when the head of Isaiah's cock pushed inside. I clenched around him involuntarily, and he paused.

"I'm okay," I assured him.

He glided in slowly, an inch at a time, waiting for me to relax with each push. It took more concentration than I thought I had not to squeeze at the intrusion, but the sensation of slowly being filled was delicious. I felt their cocks pressing against each other through the thin wall dividing them.

They shifted, and Kane began to thrust. Isaiah met his pace, slowly at first, and then picking up speed. I dug my fingers into Kane's chest, sinking into every new feeling. Swimming in the experience. Drowning in pleasure.

Isaiah snaked his hand between Kane and me and found my clit again. It was tender from his last visit, but he pressed hard, grinding his fingers into the inflamed flesh, pounding in my ass. I was almost hoarse when a series of cries tore from my throat, drawing out with each spike of pleasure. Holding me at the edge of orgasm and stealing my thoughts as I came. Through the haze of it all, I was aware of them thrusting, grunting, the twin sounds of them climaxing, but I wasn't sure who finished first, or how long the moment spanned.

My mind was blank when we collapsed in a pile on the bed, Isaiah tugging me to lay next to him, and Kane half under me. It would probably take some time before my limbs responded. Several minutes ticked away, before the clouds cleared from my thoughts.

The first words that managed to form in my head were, *Wow. That was amazing.* The next were, *What else have you missed out on by not asking?*

The question hovered in my mind, mingling with the euphoria of the evening, insisting it was important I listen.

Whatever I was trying to tell myself, it would wait until tomorrow.

Chapter Six

The next morning, I extracted myself from tangled limbs and climbed from the bed. The moment I was gone, Kane and Isaiah wrapped themselves around each other, neither waking. The sight warmed me and ached in a hollow pit in my chest. It was that bond again. That indescribable something the two of them radiated together. Once-in-a-lifetime, sleeping soundly in front of me.

I shook aside the thoughts and focused on more pleasant ones instead. Last night, for instance. That had been amazing. I got the impression my tastes ran pretty tame, even though to me it was almost all new and kinky. I'd enjoyed every minute of it. I grabbed my clothes and headed for the shower. That was one thing none of us considered last night. Three people on a schedule, sharing a shower, wasn't going to be easy.

Actually, more than one of us sharing at a time could be fun. My skin heated several degrees at the idea. That was one for the fantasy bin. I was tempted to let it play out in my head under the hot water, but last night left me sore and satisfied. And maybe a little reluctant to go back to finishing myself off with no one else around.

What else have you missed out on by not asking?

The question from last night careened in from nowhere, slamming into my thoughts at high speed. I turned on the water and waited for it to heat while I spun the words over in my head. Why was I so fixated on that?

I stripped down and stepped under the almost scalding shower. Would James and I still be together if I knew how to voice what I wanted? I shook the question aside before it could sour in my gut. For some reason, the only thing that hurt when I thought about him was that he'd cheated. There was no ache he was gone. No longing to get him back. That was kind of fucked up.

The loan for the cookie business. Maybe I hadn't been asking hard enough for that. Which felt ridiculous. I had a business plan, three-year profit-and-loss projections, and financial statements proving the idea made money. I went into each bank meeting professionally.

And still, every single person told me they didn't see a long-term future in hand-painted cookie bouquets with videogame people on them.

The thoughts swirled in my head, none of them giving me any answers. I shut the water off, dried, dressed, and brushed my hair. And… the guys were asleep. I should wake them, but they'd driven for two days straight, it was only eight, and Vegas was less than ten hours away. They could sleep a little longer. Maybe I'd mock up some new cookie designs.

My phone vibrated, startling me, when I grabbed it from the top of my duffel back. I laughed quietly at my own jumpiness and checked the message.

Call me in five minutes, or I'm sending the cops to your phone's GPS location. It was from Julie.

Crap. I sent Kane and Isaiah a text saying I'd be in the diner, grabbed my laptop, and dialed Julie as I strolled out the motel room door.

"Where the hell are you?"

I had to hold the phone several inches from my ear, to keep from going deaf at the volume of her question. I brought the device back to my head and adopted my most apologetic voice. "I'm sorry. I completely forgot when we got in last night." I left off the bit about being focused on other things. Julie had a hard enough time understanding how I flirted with Kane and Isaiah when they *weren't* standing in front of me. I'd fill her in the moment I got home.

"Swear to me you're okay." Julie's tone quieted enough it only half drilled into my eardrums.

"I'm fine. I promise. No one's holding me hostage or forcing me to say that. They're both heavy sleepers."

"How can you be fine?" Julie asked. "That asshole you were dating was fucking another woman."

I winced at the reminder, but the empty pit I should feel about him being gone still wasn't there. "I promise I'm good, the guys aren't serial killers, and I'll survive the next week with them."

"All right." Julie sighed. "I'm just worried. As soon as you get home, ice cream and movies with zombies?"

I grimaced. Fake gore nauseated me, but Julie loved picking the films apart and deciding what the survivors had done right and wrong. "Action with lots of explosions. I'm the one who's heartbroken, remember?" But was I?

"Yeah, all right. Text me when you get to Vegas, and again when you leave. And if you win that ten-thousand-dollar prize, bring me something pretty."

"We're not going to win, but I'll find you something anyway. Laters."

I dropped my phone in my purse and made my way into the diner. I snagged a table for three, with the disclaimer the other two might be a while, and a request to keep the coffee coming in the meantime. The place was mostly empty. A couple of men in suits and ties sat alone at their tables, one staring at a phone and the other flipping through a newspaper. Perfect atmosphere for drawing.

I set up my laptop and grabbed my stylus. The machine had cost me a small fortune. It was powerful enough to game on, and also had a touch screen so I could draw and design on it. I purchased it about four months ago, using profits from cookie sales. James had freaked out, demanding to know how I could justify almost five grand on a stupid fucking computer.

Asshole.

I pulled up a clean screen and started to sketch. I lost track of time as I bled together colors and lines. My mind drifted easily from one *nothing* topic to the next. Once I got the design solid, I'd be able to reproduce it quickly on each cookie. One of our selling points was I painted them all by hand—probably not practical, but I could do one in about five minutes. It was getting the prototype to a stage I was comfortable reproducing that took the most time.

"Wow. You're amazing." Isaiah's comment startled me.

I let out a tiny squeak and dropped my stylus. A line smeared across the screen. Fuck. I undid the error, grateful it didn't take any of my work with it, and saved the image before stowing my laptop.

"Didn't mean to sneak up on you. Sorry." He slid into the booth across from me.

I was surprised, but didn't complain when Kane took the seat next to me instead. He might have done it so he could talk face to face with Isaiah, but I liked the occasional brush of his arm against mine.

"He's right. You're fantastic," Kane said. "You're freehanding that, without a reference image or anything."

The compliments flushed me. I reached for my coffee—something to hide my lack of response behind—and realized the cup was empty. I settled on replying with, "You've both seen my cookies before."

"You could be doing more." Kane grabbed the pot the waitress had left on the table, and refilled my cup. "Design work. Something commercial-art based."

"I could. But I like doing this. It's fun. Julie makes amazing cookies, and this is an excuse to work with my best friend." Who I'd shrugged off twice in the last couple of days, and to whom I completely neglected to even drop hints about what happened last night. I'd have to make it up to her when I got home.

Isaiah didn't look as awake and alert as Kane. Sunglasses hid his eyes, and he yawned every few seconds. "If you like it, keep doing it."

"What he said." Kane traced a finger down my arm. "You could have waited for us to shower this morning."

I couldn't help the pleased flutter that his teasing echoed my earlier thoughts. "Maybe next time."

"I'll remember you said that."

My laugh died in my throat, as it occurred to me that, after what happened last night, I had no idea if he was serious.

An hour later, we were caffeinated, awake, and on the road again. Isaiah drove. Kane insisted I sit up front, and took the seat behind me. We were discussing whether or not Boba Fett died like a punk in *Return of the Jedi.* Opinions on the subject were mixed. We finally agreed that was Mace Windu's fate.

Kane leaned forward and rested his arm on mine, intertwining our fingers. The sudden intimate touch sent a glow spreading from my chest into my limbs. It felt a lot nicer than it probably should.

"Have you ever done it in a car before?" he asked.

My cheeks were already warm from the summer sun striking me through glass, so at least I had an excuse for any flush on my face. "Thrown Boba Fett into a sarlacc pit?" I knew what he meant, but it felt easier to laugh it off than acknowledge it.

Isaiah glanced at me, then turned his attention back to the road, a tiny smirk playing on his face.

"No," Kane said. "Sex. Have you ever had sex in a car before?"

There wasn't so much room for misinterpretation there. "Not at seventy miles an hour."

"So, stopped?"

Apparently, the concept of inexperience still wasn't clicking with them. "No, not even stopped."

"We'll have to fix that, then."

I opened my mouth to reply, but no answer was forthcoming. Wit, deflection, agreement—what was right? I wanted to say, *Okay.*

Isaiah glanced at me again. "What's wrong?"

"I don't know." I sank back into my seat. "I guess… after last night, I don't know where the line is anymore. Are you teasing? Serious? Something I can't fathom?"

Kane tugged my ponytail. "You just have to ask."

"I kind of feel like a wet blanket that way. You know, like making someone explain a joke."

"It's not the same. If you want to know, just ask me."

I didn't agree that I should have to. It felt awkward. But I did want an answer. "In that case, are you serious about the sex in a car?"

"Absolutely. If you'd let me, I'd pull you back here right now, and we could cover the car and the seventy-mile-an-hour achievements at the same time."

"It's not a video game." Irritation sparked Isaiah's voice. "And some of us have to pay attention to the road."

His tone was enough to keep me from drawing more conclusions. Regardless of how serious Kane was, I didn't want to piss off either of them, or be the reason for them fighting.

"Sorry." Kane sounded anything but. "We'll talk about baseball instead."

I made a face. "Really? I guess I can see how hitting balls with a bat could be a mood killer, but baseball?"

Isaiah glanced over. "Pod racing, then."

"That's more like it." I was happy to let the conversation slide to more neutral ground, but I couldn't get the teasing, or the implication it meant more, out of my head. I felt like I was missing a bigger picture. Big enough that it didn't matter if I was comfortable asking.

I didn't know the right question.

Chapter Seven

"I have a reservation for James Whitner," I told the man at the hotel registration desk. I hated the taste of *his* name rolling off my tongue, but he booked the room.

"Of course. I just need your ID and a credit card." He was already typing.

I slid the cards across the desk. He looked between my driver's license and his screen, and frowned. He punched a few more keys. "I'll be right back." He didn't make eye contact. Impatience flitted through me, and I squashed it. This wasn't his fault. At least I'd remembered to text Julie when we got into town, so she wouldn't be waiting if this took all day.

"Everything all right?" Isaiah stepped up next to me.

An uneasy feeling clenched in my gut. "I

think so." I hoped so.

Several minutes passed, before the clerk returned and handed back my stuff. "I'm sorry, miss, the room isn't in your name. I can't check you in."

"What?" Irritation flared inside, and I swallowed it back. This wasn't his fault. Options ticked through my head. "Then give me another room."

"We're booked full, thanks to the competition. We don't even have any free comp rooms. Unless you're spending more than a thousand dollars a night at the tables."

Crap. I shoved my cards back in my purse. Shit. Fuck. What now? I fumbled for any alternative at all. "Do you have a waiting list or something?"

"Not that will do you any good. I'm sorry." He glanced behind me. "Next, please."

Apparently the conversation was over. I stepped aside, thoughts racing. I'd go online. Hit up hotel websites. They couldn't all be booked. This was the strip. Fifty conventions in town, but there would still be a room somewhere, right?"

Isaiah moved in front of me, sympathy in his eyes. "Stay in our room. We've got a big bed."

The idea was entirely too appealing, but that was the last thing I needed. I had to keep in mind last night had been about learning to go after what I wanted, which didn't include getting in the middle of their relationship. "I can sleep in a chair. Or have them send up a roll-away."

"Dee, don't." Isaiah's tone was firm. "We have to be in top form for the competition, right? Share the bed with us."

45

I didn't want to refuse anyway. I felt a little dim for not being able to guess how far they wanted to take things, though.

No, I didn't. I forced the words through my thoughts. We'd established ground rules last night. They were very clear about the fact it was no strings. A way to help me move past a couple insecurities. I wasn't going to be the girl who was so inexperienced, she saw things that weren't there. I wouldn't ruin our friendship or their relationship because I couldn't separate sex from emotions. They were being friendly, the way they'd always been online, and I needed to stop reading more into it. "Okay. Offer accepted."

"Good." He rested a hand at the small of my back and pointed me toward the elevators. "We'll get settled, hit early registration, and go grab some dinner."

"Absolutely." I fell into step between them, trying with every ounce of reason I could muster to ignore the spike of want spreading from his palm through my spine.

"Andrea." A familiar voice sliced through me, filling my veins with ice.

I clenched my teeth and spun, to find James standing a few feet behind me. I didn't know what to say, though *fuck off and die* lingered on the tip of my tongue.

"I'm glad you're here after all." He stepped forward, smile warm and friendly.

"Dee?" Isaiah's kneaded my back, his fingers reassuring and hot compared to the sensations filling the rest of me.

James glanced between the two guys. "Your gaming friends, right? Thanks for getting her here safe." He held out a room key. "I checked us in already. Let's go upstairs and talk."

Kane stepped forward, and I grabbed his wrist. "No." I was surprised at the venom in my own tone. "I won't."

"Just let me explain. The other night, I—"

"Stop." I clenched my jaw so hard it ached, but it was the only way to keep from shaking with anger. "We're not talking. There's nothing to discuss. You can rot in hell, for all I care." The words felt good spilling past my lips.

"You misunderstood." Pleading mixed with condescension leaked into his tone. I was impressed and mildly disgusted he pulled off both at the same time.

Kane pulled free of my grip and slammed his palm into James's chest, knocking him back a few steps. "Tell her which part she misunderstood." Heads turned in our direction. "The part where you were buried balls deep in another woman?" Kane took another step forward, and James moved back. "Or the part where you fucking deluding yourself into thinking you were good enough for her?"

"This is between me and Andrea, asshole."

Kane growled. "Don't call her that." He clenched his hands into fists.

Two gentlemen in hotel shirts stepped between them, both broader in the shoulders than Isaiah, with jaws as square as my laptop. "Is there a problem, gentlemen?" one asked.

"No, sir. We're just on our way to our room."

Kane stepped back, hands up, palms out. "He just kind of attacked my girlfriend. Started calling her someone else's name, talking crazy. I don't know."

The other one turned to James. "Sir?"

"Fuck…" James growled. "Andrea, just fucking talk me."

Security guard one looked at me. "Is that you?"

"No." I shook my head. "I'm Andi. I don't know who this guy is."

"Fucking bitch." James surged forward.

Guard two pushed him back. "We're going to have to ask you to leave, sir." He looked at me. "Very sorry for the trouble, miss."

"Of course." I gave him a sweet smile. My pulse raced a million miles a minute, as they escorted James from the building. I should feel bad about that, but a strange elation spilled through me.

"Come on." Isaiah guided me toward the elevator again.

A million words and ideas and emotions jumbled in my head, as we rode up to our floor, and I couldn't make sense of them. I was grateful neither of them spoke. I needed to sort out the mess of thoughts. James actually followed me here. To apologize.

Which seemed sweet, until I considered he hadn't called. He hadn't texted or emailed. He'd fucking ambushed me in a public place, after stealing my room. And the way Kane had stepped forward… But it wasn't just him. Isaiah stood by my side the entire time. *She's my girlfriend.* Kane's voice echoed in my head. I didn't like the sound of that. Not in the least. Who was I kidding? I loved the sound of it.

We reached our floor and made our way to the room. I followed the appropriate motions as we stepped inside, but I was stuck in my head.

It had only been two days—forty-eight hours—since I'd walked in on my boyfriend fucking someone else. Since I decided to drive halfway across the country, with two guys I only knew from an online game. Since I surrendered everything smart and logical and reasonable, in order to escape that single sight.

And the only bit of it I regretted was the nagging question— *why did I ever stay with James for so long?*

What the hell was wrong with me?

"Hey." Isaiah waved a hand in front of my face, drawing me out of my trance. "Are you in there?"

The single question snapped something inside. A dam I didn't recognize until it broke. I tried to find an answer, but all that came out was a sob.

Isaiah gathered me in his arms, and I buried my head in his chest. He didn't say anything, just trailed his fingers through my hair.

I cried. I couldn't stop. I bled out every frustration in a wash of tears, and then forced out more. What was I doing?

Chapter Eight

Isaiah held me until I managed to bring the tears under control. He was like a cuddly, well-muscled, blue-eyed teddy bear. Kane brought me a glass of water and knelt on the floor next to where we sat on the bed.

"Can you talk about it?" There was no pressure in Isaiah's question, only concern.

I dragged in a shaky breath. "I can probably form words, if that's what you mean." My voice came out a dry rasp. I felt guilty, with both of them hovering over me. I didn't think I'd ever been pampered like this in my entire life, even though all they did was listen to and comfort me.

Isaiah pulled back enough to look at me, and brushed a few tears from my face. "Did you ever actually mourn, after you walked out on him, or was it straight to the champagne?"

"I cried in a grocery-store parking lot." I pulled several tissues from the box on the nightstand and tried to wipe more of the grief from my cheeks. "God, you must think I'm pathetic."

"Why would we?" Isaiah asked.

"I wasn't good enough to keep a boyfriend. I can't convince anyone to loan me money for my business, even though the thing makes a good profit. The only way I can get laid is—" I clamped my mouth shut, not sure what I'd been about to say but knowing it wouldn't make things better.

Kane shifted to sit on the bed behind me, draped an arm over my shoulder, and pulled me until I sat in his lap. "We shouldn't have pushed you."

"You didn't. I wanted it. I just…"

"What?" Isaiah drew my attention again.

"There has to be something wrong with me. The only reason I'm miserable about James is that I didn't see it coming. That I convinced myself I was happy with him. Who does that? Who walks away from a six-month relationship and doesn't sink into depression for at least a little while? And instead, I'm glad he's gone. I'm relieved I'm here with the two of you instead of him, cheating asshole or not."

Kane rested his chin on my shoulder and leaned his head against mine. The simple gesture was more reassuring than any words. I wasn't going to read into it. It just felt nice.

Isaiah stroked a thumb over the back of my knuckles. "There's nothing wrong with you."

"So why are you trying to change me?" The question sounded childish to my ears. It certainly wasn't fair to shovel that on them.

"No." Isaiah furrowed his brow and paused, as if searching for the right words. "That's not the point. I don't want you to change. I want you to be more comfortable with who you are."

"Who I am isn't comfortable with all this speaking-my-mind bullshit." I was being a brat. Besides, my objection didn't feel right. It tasted like deception, rolling off my tongue.

"Then you don't have to. I know who you are online, though. In chat. When we go head-to-head with a team of guys giving you shit because you're a girl, you don't back down, and you never hesitate. Not to fire, and not to tell them where to stick it. But"— Isaiah tugged my fingers—"if you don't like any of this, don't do it. Simple as that."

His observations caught me off-guard. I'd never seen myself that way. Online I was just…being the person I couldn't be in real life. Damn. He was right. I gave him a hesitant smile. "I like it more than I probably should."

"No such thing." One corner of his mouth tugged up. "Feeling better?"

"Not completely. I still feel a little stupid for breaking down, but I think I have my head on straighter than it's been in a few days."

Kane squeezed me. "Good. To the last bit. The rest will come with time. No regrets?"

"None."

"Perfect." Isaiah grabbed the hotel menu from the nightstand and flopped it open on the bed. "Now we splurge and order room service, and rent the stupidest movie we can find."

"You know that stuff costs a fortune, right?"

"Don't care." He flipped to the appetizers. "We're on vacation."

I could do this. Spending time with my friends. Taking it easy. No pressure.

****

It was amazing what a full night of sleep could do. It didn't hurt that I'd been pinned between two gorgeous guys. In a completely platonic way, of course. Waking up with Kane's hand on my stomach, under my shirt, and his erection pressing into my butt, was just a hazard of sharing a bed with guys. A delicious, tempting hazard.

"What are you daydreaming about?" Isaiah nudged me down an aisle crowded with seated gamers and their computers.

I almost said *nothing,* but my good mood, combined with my revelation from last night, didn't want to hold back. Still, this wasn't the time or place. "Later, I promise."

"Holding you to that." Kane gestured toward a block of three empty seats about halfway down the row. "I think that's us." Even though the competition wouldn't start for almost twenty minutes, the room already rumbled with the thousands of voices.

We squeezed ourselves into the spot designated for us, and set up. It was a good thing we all had headsets; even sitting next to each other, we wouldn't be able to hear once things started. Everyone in the room—a thousand teams of three each—would be barking orders at each other.

Though the three of us had never done this in

close quarters before, we needed little discussion to figure out who sat where and how we wanted everything plugged in. In a few minutes, we were set. Nervous excitement thrummed through me. We had a snowball's chance in Hell of winning, but the energy in the room, the fact we were here, was like a contact high.

"Excuse me." A strong voice cut through the bedlam, and someone tapped me on the arm.

I whirled and found myself staring into the most emerald green eyes I'd ever seen. Still didn't hold a candle to Isaiah's blue, but the guy was cute. "Hi?"

"Hey." He grinned. "I was wondering… One of our guys lost his USB lightning cable. Any chance you have a spare?"

"Uh, yeah." I dug through my bag and produced one seconds later.

"Thanks." He grabbed it and nodded several rows over. "I'll bring it back tonight. We're in green thirty-two, though, in case I forget." He hesitated. "Good luck." And then he flowed back into the crowd.

Behind me, Kane snorted. "*In case I forget.* He won't forget."

I turned back to face him and Isaiah, eyebrows raised in question. "Why do you say that?"

Isaiah dropped into his chair. "He swam through three rows of people, to ask you specifically if he could borrow a cable. You don't think he asked every other person before you?"

"Maybe." I hadn't thought about it, but now they'd pointed it out, it seemed obvious.

"So you found your grudge-fuck guy." Kane turned away, to fiddle with something on his laptop.

The words sank heavy in my gut and drilled a tiny hole in my mood. Not that I had any right to be upset. He was only pointing out what we all already knew. "Yeah. I guess so."

"*Weak!*" The exclamation was close enough to carry above all the other noise. "I'm not playing against a fucking girl."

I rolled my eyes and turned in the direction of the complaint. The guy stood on the other side of the tables we set up on. At least this, I was prepared to deal with. I adopted an exaggerated pout. "What's wrong with girls?"

He hesitated. That never happened online. Then again, this was the first time I'd ever looked a troll in the eye.

His friends nudged him, and his expression hardened. "Besides the fact you can't play?"

I raised my brows. "Then it's an easy win for you, right?"

One of his buddies elbowed him, and he said, "Besides, if it's that time of the month, you'll probably start crying when you lose."

I caught my bottom lip between my teeth, hoping it looked more flirty and innocent than silly. "It's not. But you're right. Win or lose, I will be screaming in ecstasy when the day is over." I leaned in and dropped my voice to a stage whisper. If we were in game, I wouldn't hesitate to say this, and while it was crass, it tended to be one of the few things that made a guy like him pause. "Do you and your hand have a similar date?"

"Stupid bitch." He turned away with a scowl. "I'll fucking kill you."

The threat didn't faze me. This was pre-game trash talk, and our team was solid. Besides, our trip wouldn't be ruined by losing. It might be a bit of a bummer, but we had the entire weekend here either way. "Not if I see you first."

"Players, take your places." A voice boomed over the PA. "Round one starts in ten minutes. Anyone not active when the timer reaches one, forfeits."

I blew the team across from us a kiss. "Good luck, boys."

Kane, Isaiah, and I settled into our seats, turned on our headsets, and did a quick sound check to make sure we heard each other and didn't get any cross-chatter. My fingers twitched on my mouse, excitement and adrenaline flooding me. Chance of a lifetime, even if we only lasted one game. This was it.

Chapter Nine

The game worked on a sudden-death principal. Five teams of three competed in arena mode, and if a player died, they were out. Last team with a player standing went to the next round.

We slid into an ordered, practiced formation as soon as we saw the map. Isaiah knew which spots held sniper rifles, and from there which locations were prime for their use. Kane would go for the shotgun, grenades, and rocket launcher. His job was to watch our backs and blow up anyone who got too close.

I didn't want a fancy weapon, but I had my fingers crossed for specialty gear. Depending on where I spawned, first goal was a pistol, and if luck was on my side, the cloaking body armor. I'd sneak up on people.

The timer counted down on screen, we

materialized in our spots, and it was time to go. Two familiar voices snapped their intentions in my ear, and I responded with the same. The next two hours were a series of *Heading North. Factory*, and *fifty meters behind you, bare handed, got him*, and *sniper, south corner base, on it*.

With so many players still alive, we saw a limited number of dots on the radar. Our own team, and anyone within weapon range of one of us. Once there were fewer than five people on the map, we'd see everyone who wasn't cloaked. That person would phase in and out regardless, and only when they were near another player.

"Behind you, Andi." Kane's warning sounded at the same time a blip appeared on my radar.

I spun my camera in time to catch the shimmer of someone cloaking, and fired into the cloud. The body reappeared, and my kill count notched by one. "Nailed it."

In a more casual game, we'd joke and toss back and forth crude innuendo. This wasn't that game. It required more focus than I'd put into anything but my art in ages. I raided my kill for his armor but didn't turn on its cloak function when I donned it. That would wait.

A freckling of red dots appeared around Isaiah.

"On our way," Kane said, and I broke into a sprint.

We were too far away, though.

"*Fuck!*" Isaiah's frustration rocked my eardrums, and our team counter dropped by one.

"No, no, no." Kane kept up his run to Isaiah's location.

"Don't. Fall back on Andi."

"Fuck that. There are almost two teams up there."

Almost. "Isaiah, how many did you get?" I asked.

"Two."

And there were three left. Kane could tag all with a single grenade if he timed it right… Which he almost always did.

But if these were two full teams, one player was hiding. "Kane, stop." I ducked inside a doorway on the roof, where Isaiah's body lay.

"Too late." Kane sounded smug as he tossed the grenade. The explosion filled the screen, and a flash sparked in the background. His kill count grew by three, at the same time our team ticker fell to one.

"Shit." My heart hammered in my chest and my pulse threatened to tear from my veins. "Sniper."

"Yeah, I got that." Kane sounded frustrated and annoyed. "Sorry, Andi."

"S'all good." I headed in the direction of the flash that had taken Kane out. The guy wouldn't be there anymore, but he could only get so far in limited directions.

A chime sounded in my headset, over the game-world sound system, and the screen lit up with five dots—four red ones and me. Everyone else was dead. Seconds later, one dot vanished, and then another blipped out. The world body count rose by one. The other person had to have a set of cloaked armor. And was probably the sniper who set up the ambush that got my team.

I clenched my toes and narrowed my gaze at the screen. I wasn't sure which missing player was dead and which was hidden, but I had enough time to get to one of the other remaining first. Another player registered dead, leaving three of us. Two visible on the map. Cloaked-guy would have to draw within weapon range for me to get a hint of his location.

Which would be soon enough. I was taking a risk that cloaked-guy would close on our location, rather than waiting for us to come to him. I counted off about how long it would take to reach us from where he'd been, and then darted in front of visible-guy, drawing his fire, and rolling behind various bits of cover to avoid being hit.

Before I reappeared from behind the car hiding me, I hit my cloak effect. I aimed, and picked off visible-guy. Our radar signatures should have vanished from the screen within seconds of each other. Now I was the only player on my map, and cloaked-guy should be seeing the same thing.

I took my second huge risk in the last few minutes, and dropped my secondary weapon. I only had a few bullets left in my pistol, so if I ran out, I was screwed. But he wouldn't see my signature until I was within my weapon's range, meaning punching distance. I just had to hope he wasn't doing the same thing.

I didn't dare look away from my screen—the outside world was a blur in my peripheral vision. The only sound I heard was the ringing in my ears, from straining too hard to listen to the digital world. My heart slammed against my ribs so hard, I was pretty sure both would be numb soon.

A flicker caught my attention on the map, and I whirled my camera toward it. Against a far wall, the glimmer of a cloaked figure hugged the brick. He skirted the area.

I crouched low and circled around behind him. I swore my eardrums might burst from the pounding of my pulse. As I drew within shooting distance of my invisible target, I said a quick prayer he wasn't facing my direction. Just as I switched from bare-handed to gun, I saw enough movement to know his weapon was coming up.

I fired faster, the sound echoing in my headphones and my skull. The in-game alarm blipped, indicating I was the final player. I blinked at the screen in disbelief, trying to process what had just happened.

An external, "Bullshit," drew me from the game. The guy who'd tried to troll us earlier.

"*Yeah!*" I tore off my headset and let it clatter onto the table. Elation filled me, painting what had to be a huge grin on my face.

Isaiah pulled me into a tight hug, lifting my feet off the ground for a moment. "You were incredible." He turned to Kane and kissed him deeply.

An unexpected heat flushed my skin at their public display of affection. Not because it embarrassed me, but wow, that was hot. I wondered if anyone around us felt the same, but the rest of the room was too lost in their own games, joy, or mourning to pay attention to us. Isaiah's fingers tangled in Kane's hair. Kane cupping Isaiah's face, holding him hostage as the moment stretched on.

"Fucking brilliant." Kane was breathless when they broke apart. I wasn't sure if he was talking about the kiss, or the fact we'd made it to the next round. "Where are we going to celebrate?"

"There's supposed to be this little hole-in-the-wall Mexican place off the strip, with killer authentic food." Isaiah wrapped an arm around both our waists. A shadow passed over Kane's face, but vanished so quickly I could have imagined it.

We tossed ideas back and forth while we grabbed our passes for tomorrow's round, and then headed into the hotel lobby. We decided on Isaiah's initial suggestion. "Drive or walk?" he asked.

"Fifteen fucking cities, hundreds of proposals, how is it this hard to find unique desserts?" The irritated voice cut through our banter.

I turned toward the complaint, and shock combined with a heavy dose of fangirling raced through me. Every other thought evaporated from my mind. I knew the guy standing about fifteen feet away, not just because he hosted one of those cooking TV shows. Dante Larson was also a well-known investor in the bakery business. If he bought into a concept, he was willing to pour thousands and hundreds of thousands into the idea, to make sure the business took off and he recouped his investment.

"Dee?" Isaiah tugged my hand. "You in there?"

"I… It's just…" I nodded toward the guy.

"Oh, hey. He's that cooking dude." Kane's

62

voice was loud enough heads turned in our direction.

Isaiah nudged me forward, and I dug my feet in, to keep from letting him propel me. "Go talk to him," he said.

I shook my head. Mr. Larson was obviously irritated, and the last thing he wanted was another fan, begging for his attention. "He's checking in for the night. I can't bother him."

"Dee."

"Forget it." I spun away. "We're celebrating." It wasn't as if I'd walk up to him and shake his hand, and he'd fund my business. If I was just going to say *hi,* for a picture or something, it could wait until he wasn't so tired and cranky. Still, it took more effort than I expected to ignore the screaming in my skull not to walk away from this.

Chapter Ten

We were all laughing and swapping jokes when we got back to the room a few hours later. The rush of making it to the next round still flowed between us. Kane flopped into a chair near the window and sprawled out, as if nothing in the world could disrupt his mood. "What now?"

They both turned toward me. "Um…" I racked my brain for an answer. If I were home and had a free night, I'd get online and talk to them. Maybe we'd all go blow some stuff up, but just as likely we'd chat. And before James, the odds were high that talk would become cyber-sex. "What would you do if I weren't here?"

The look they shared answered my question. Heat filled my veins and rolled over my skin, as images flooded into my thoughts. *Drop it.* Pushing this boundary wasn't appropriate. But the fantasy wouldn't leave me alone. It flitted through my mind and tingled in my fingertips and taunted me with a need for more. I trusted them to tell me if I crossed a line. I realized two pairs of eyes were on me. "Would you still consider *celebrating* with me here?"

Isaiah dragged his gaze over my body, leaving goosebumps in its wake. "Feels a little awkward, if only two of us are enjoying ourselves."

That almost sounded like a *yes*. It certainly wasn't a *no*. Desire tightened through my body, and my nipples strained against my bra. I wanted to strip it off while I watched them. Relieve the tension. "You wouldn't be the only ones."

Kane raised his brows and sat straight up in the chair.

Isaiah placed a finger at the base of my throat and traced down my torso. "So, while we're celebrating, you'll be watching and enjoying? Playing with yourself? Getting off to the sight of us?" A heavy undercurrent ran through his voice and danced over my nerves.

A throb spread between my thighs. "That's what I'm hoping for."

"I like the way you think." Kane stood, closed the distance between us, and spun Isaiah to face him. He gripped Isaiah's face between his palms and kissed him hard, twin groans tearing through the room.

I sank onto the mattress, attention fixed on the men. Every grunt or grab or shift of their bodies against each other raised my arousal. It wasn't just the physical contact—the way Isaiah stripped off Kane's shirt, then dug his fingers into Kane's chest hard enough indentations appeared around his grip, or that Kane held Isaiah captive, biting his lips, devouring his mouth. The turn-on was how into it they were. How much both of them enjoyed it.

Isaiah moved his hands lower. Kane thrust his hips forward when Isaiah reached his waist. Each new movement felt as if it happened to me.

I pushed up my shirt and caressed my breasts through my bra. The line between what I felt and what I watched blurred in my mind, and I dove into both real and imagined sensations.

Isaiah unbuckled Kane's belt, undid the button on his jeans, and pulled down the zipper. When he shoved Kane's clothes to the ground, I wanted it to be me, kneeling, wrapping my hand around Kane's shaft, making him groan and lean into me. Feeling his hard flesh in my palm while I stroked.

I had too many clothes on. I stripped off my shirt and bra. My nipples were already rigid, eager peaks, hot against the cool air of the room. I pinched them and twisted between my fingers. When Kane's gaze met mine, my pulse spiked.

"Enjoying the show?" His voice was strained. He let out a long moan when Isaiah dropped to his knees and flicked his tongue over the head of Kane's cock.

"God, yes." I could almost taste the salty drop of precum. I squeezed my breasts harder, and a steady beat between my legs begged for attention.

Isaiah took Kane's entire length into his mouth. Kane sucked in a breath, teeth clenched, and tangled his fingers in Isaiah's hair, holding him captive.

If I were watching porn on my computer, I'd strip the rest of my clothes off right now, and finger myself until I came. The goal would be getting off and moving on. I wanted to see this through to the end, though. Hold out until they neared the finish line.

"Play with yourself," Kane said.

I wasn't sure which of us he was talking to. The moment I slid my fingers between my folds, I wouldn't be able to stop.

The sound of my zipper mingled with Isaiah's. I kicked my jeans off while I watched him work his dick free. Geez, that was hot. He continued to suck and lick Kane, while he stroked himself at the same pace, slowly building up the rhythm.

I glided one hand over my panties, still squeezing a nipple with the other. Tiny gasps filtered from my throat.

Kane's breathing grew shallow, and he studied me. "I want to see your pussy, Andi. Spread yourself open and get yourself off while you watch us."

As if spurred on by the words, Isaiah sped up, head bobbing against Kane, hand jerking himself faster.

I hadn't meant to become part of the show. This was supposed to be me watching them, living the high through them. But I liked the way Kane stared at me. I could lose myself in the images of what it would be like to be in front of him, while I was still here, playing with myself.

I tried to be seductive about dragging off my

underwear. Whether or not I managed, I saw Kane tighten his grip on Isaiah's hair. I stroked my slit. I was wetter than I ever remembered being, moisture coating the inside of my thighs. My clit begged for attention, but I didn't dare. Not yet. I pushed two fingers inside myself. My gasps and whimpers blended with theirs. I didn't dare take my gaze off the show. It was too much a part of everything I felt.

"Fuck." Kane's movements were. "Can you come like that, Andi?"

I never had before. Not from penetration alone. But every sensation—direct or observed—rolling over me pushed another button of pleasure. "Maybe."

He clenched his jaw, and a loud groan tore from his chest. "Fuck yourself till you do. I want to hear you scream in pleasure again." His words were stuttered with short grabs for air.

Isaiah grunted around the dick in his mouth, and stroked himself faster.

Kane closed his eyes and leaned back his head. My skin felt like it was on fire—a more incredible, erotic heat than I thought possible. I plunged inside myself, bumping my clit with my palm and kneading my breast until spikes of agonizing pleasure shot through me, tugging at an invisible cord. I teetered on the edge, not quite able to finish, and not wanting to stop.

Kane bucked hips against Isaiah's face, hard and punctuated. Orgasm spilled over me, rolling in hard waves, as I clenched around my hand. Kane's groans dragged into a single, long sound, and then he shuddered to a stop.

Isaiah still yanked his own cock as he kissed and licked and pulled away from Kane. Each new flick of Isaiah's tongue made Kane shudder again.

I eased off, sinking into the heady euphoria that danced at the edges of my thoughts. *Wow.* I wasn't sure if I spoke the word or it was just that loud in my head.

Kane fell to his knees, at eye-level with Isaiah, then crushed their mouths together. My ebbing pleasure surged back full force at the hunger in the kiss. At the thought of Kane tasting himself on someone else's lips. He covered Isaiah's hand, both of them stroking while he deepened the kiss.

I didn't have any more restraint. I moved my fingers to my clit, finding the swollen button with ease.

Isaiah tugged his cock as he groaned into Kane's mouth. I could taste the kiss. I rubbed my clit harder, grinding against my hand, climax building past the bursting point inside. I whimpered when I came a second time. Pushing myself until I couldn't take my own touch. My head was light, drifting like a balloon, as I watched the sight in front of me. As if my orgasm pushed Isaiah over the edge, he gave his dick several more hard jerks before shudders ran through him.

Kane rested his forehead against Isaiah's and let out a strained chuckle. They kissed again, and I ducked my head. Regardless of what I'd just witnessed and my near-participation, this moment felt too intimate for spectators.

An ache spread in my chest. I was falling for two men who loved each other more than anything.

Falling. The word tumbled through my thoughts. Where had that come from? And both? Really? I couldn't be. I didn't know what that felt like. I'd confused sex with love. Further proof that, if I was going to do something like get my brains screwed out to get over James, I should be doing it with a stranger. Someone I didn't already have an emotional attachment to. Someone who wasn't already head-over-heels for another person.

Chapter Eleven

The guys were still sleeping when I woke the next morning. Kane's arm was draped over my stomach, Isaiah spooned behind him. A raw edge gripped my throat, and I struggled to swallow it down. Sure, my friendship with them had contained an assumed *with benefits* clause since the first time we cybered but they were still *just* friends. I needed to remember that.

I extracted myself from them as carefully as I could, not in the mood for either an awkward conversation or glossing over the situation. Both sounded more painful than I could deal with.

The plan was to shower, leave them a note, and tiptoe out of here before they woke up. Maybe a little time alone would help me screw my head on straight before the next competition round. I pulled off Part One without a hitch, but when I stepped from the bathroom, Kane and Isaiah sat next to each other on the bed, talking quietly.

Kane looked up, and his gaze lingered on me for a moment before he said, "You should have waited for us."

"In the shower?" I wasn't sure what to make of the comment. Was it common for no-strings sex to happen at every available opportunity? That seemed a bit much. A snippet of me asked if maybe he was interested in more, but that was ridiculous. He had a wonderful boyfriend, and he'd made it really clear yesterday that he thought I'd do well to hook up with USB-cable-guy.

"Unless you were somewhere else right now." Kane winked, and a smirk played on his face.

What was I supposed to say? Nothing rude or defensive. Not that I felt either one. I'd rather he was serious. The bravado I'd found amid the rush of winning last night had faded this morning. "I'm not sure the shower is big enough for three people."

"We could have found a way."

As much as I wanted to fall into the teasing casually, and not have it mean anything, I wasn't there right now. "There's plenty of room for two. You can still enjoy yourselves."

"Dee." Isaiah scooted the edge of the bed.

I stepped out of his reach and placed my hand on the doorknob. "I'm going souvenir hunting for Julie. Find me when you're ready for breakfast."

I was out the door and heading toward the elevator before I could second-guess my decision. The last thing I wanted to hear right now was some sort of obligatory reassurance. Scattered thoughts bounced in my head as I made my way downstairs. In one direction, slot machines and video poker taunted the casual wanderer. *Just drop in a quarter,* their chimes summoned. I'd have to go through that, to find the real souvenir shops and probably for us to grab breakfast. That was okay. The siren song didn't tempt me, but the flashing lights might distract me.

Even though I'd barely been a remote participant last night, I felt more a part of the shared moment than I ever had, sleeping with James. The energy in the room last night… And the fact that, even though Kane watched me, it was between them. Shared atmosphere or not, I was still the awkward third wheel on their bike. I wasn't supposed to get attached. The frustration played on repeat, dancing to the jangling bells, until I thought I'd have to scream to make it stop. I wasn't sure how long I wandered the rows, sucked into the mire of frustration.

"Hey, Andi."

I didn't recognize the voice, but he obviously knew me. As long as it wasn't James, I was grateful for the chance to step outside my head. I spun and found myself face to face with the USB-cable guy from yesterday. A bitter wash of indecision filled me. I wanted to be pleased he knew my name, but Kane's voice echoed in my skull. *You just found your grudge-fuck guy.*

I wanted to snarl at the invisible words. Instead, I gave the guy a smile. "Hey, uh…"

"Glen." He held out his hand. "I didn't expect to run into you down here."

"I know. I bet we're the only competition

73

contestants roaming the casino floors of the hotel we're all staying in." I gave him a shy smile, so he knew my sarcasm was meant to tease.

He laughed and raked his fingers through his hair. "Good point. Congratulations on your win yesterday. We were already out by the time you finished, and I saw you on the big screens. You're really good."

Heat—both pleased embarrassment and pride—flooded my face. "Thanks. I got lucky." *That should be your opening. Use the joke to ask him out.* The nagging was in Kane's voice. I couldn't force the invitation out, though.

"No. You've got skills." Glen shifted his weight from one foot to the other. At least I wasn't the only one feeling awkward. "And, um, I forgot to give back your cable yesterday. Sorry. I don't have it on me."

Say you'll go back to his room with him and get it. At least my conscience sounded more like Kane than me. That was normal, right? My already flustered insides jumbled further when I saw Kane and Isaiah weaving their way through slot machines, heading in our direction. And then I lost sight of them. "It's okay. It really was a spare."

"All right." Glen searched my face. "Then, I guess good luck in the next round."

An arm brushed my back, a familiar woodsy, clean scent seeping into my senses. Kane. "You have to ask. He's not going to." Even though he spoke quietly enough it was only meant for my ears, his voice was distinctly external. Less than a second later, his presence seemed to evaporate.

74

I didn't know if he'd still be there if I turned around. I wasn't going to look. That simple prompting cemented everything I'd struggled with. They didn't want me as more than a friend in the long run. This really was about helping me hook up with someone else. I ignored the sharp stab in my chest, and gave Glen a huge grin. "But, it would be nice to have it back. Do you want to meet up later? Like, dinner or something, after the next round?"

It wasn't quite *let's find a quiet corner and get naughty*, but that would probably scare him off as much as the idea of saying it terrified me.

Glen hesitated for a minute, then shook his head. "Sorry. I'm not used to cute girls asking me out. Or any girls. But especially gorgeous ones. I'd love to."

I ducked my head at the compliment and tried to ignore the nasty shards of hurt, spite, and dishonestly inside. If this was what Kane and Isaiah thought was best, I agreed. I couldn't stay hung up on them. A tiny whisper told me the grudge fuck was to get over James, not my best friends. Of course it was. I knew that. I kept the internal war from my face. "See you tonight, then."

He half turned, then spun back to face me and squeezed my hand. "Good luck today. I'll be watching."

He faded into the crowds, and I turned toward the shops at the other end of the casino. Two text messages waited for me. One from Isaiah with a restaurant name. The other from Kane. *I hope he said yes.*

Asshole. The word surged from nowhere and

stuck in my thoughts. I struggled to push it aside. This was nothing more than what we'd always meant it to be. Two days of screwing around didn't make a relationship, and they certainly weren't a good reason to destroy a strong friendship.

I found Isaiah and Kane already seated in a little bakery near the casino entrance. Three cups of coffee sat on the table. That one of them had ordered for me helped soothe the sting inside. Not a lot, but enough to reinforce they still cared. Just not *like that.*

Kane was on the phone, voice low, but heavy with irritation. "He already signed the lease."

Work, Isaiah mouthed.

I shrugged in understanding. Just another reminder they had lives outside of this little pocket of reality. Isaiah was an army recruiter, and Kane a rental property broker.

Kane snarled and tossed his phone on the table. It clattered against the sugar. The coffee in my mug splashed up but not over the edge.

"Fuck." A growl undercut Kane's curse.

"The property in Schaumburg?" Isaiah asked.

"Yeah. The jerk put a stop on the deposit check and wants out of the contract. I don't get it." Kane swiped his phone screen a few times, then slid it to me. "Why won't anyone take this place?"

I liked the distraction. If they were fine, I was too. I grabbed his phone and flipped through pictures and a features list. Four thousand square feet, ovens, and an industrial-size Hobart mixer. Zoned for retail and residential. I handed him back his phone. There was no reason to ask about pest infestations or structural problems. If Kane knew the place had issues like that, he wouldn't broker a deal for it. "It looks perfect to me." I meant it. "If I lived in Chicago, and Julie and I could get financing, I'd open shop there."

"Yeah. *If.* Too bad."

The edge in his tone caught me off guard and re-summoned my doubt. Or maybe I imagined I heard it. The last thing I needed was to project my doubts and insecurities on them. I forced a smile into place. "You'll make it work. I have faith in you."

He pocketed the device and rolled his eyes. "Whatever."

That time I didn't have to second-guess. Annoyance was there, and it twisted a knife in my gut. I didn't know where it came from, and his scowl discouraged me from pushing for more. My phone buzzed, and I reached for it.

"Is it grudge-fuck guy?" Kane's tone had gone from pissed off to sickly sweet.

I narrowed my eyes, wishing I had time to ask what his problem was. "It's Julie. I'll be back." I walked away from the table as I answered. Normally I wouldn't have a problem taking the call in front of them, but I didn't think I could talk to her in that atmosphere, with Kane shifting from hot to cold and back again, and Isaiah clenching his hand so hard his knuckles paled.

What was going on with us?

Chapter Twelve

"Hey." I was glad I didn't have to force the cheer into my voice with Julie. Not over this, anyway.

"You all right?"

"Fine. Just didn't sleep well last night." I'd probably tell her all about this when I got home, but right now it didn't make sense to me; there was no way I could explain it to someone else.

"Well, I have the best news, and it's going to make you feel brilliant."

I wanted her joy to be contagious. If I concentrated hard enough, I could *almost* feel it. "What's up?"

"I found the perfect place for us to set up shop." A light current ran through her tone, and I could picture her struggling to sit still, as if she were in right in front of me. "Rent's reasonable, it's in a great neighborhood, and the owner is completely gorgeous."

My mood sank further. If things had gone differently with the last loan officer—or any of them—this would be fantastic. "We don't have the money to rent a place." I wanted to add *you know that*, but it took too much effort to half-tell her no. She sounded so thrilled.

"You haven't even asked where it is. And did I mention the gorgeous guy?"

That was the last thing I needed. Another cute guy in my life. Then again, if she was interested, Julie could flirt her brains out. "Where is it?"

"Boston. Can you believe it? In that amazing old part of town we loved when we visited."

I leaned against a nearby wall and turned my gaze to the ceiling. A fresh surge of frustration welled inside. I could tell how much she wanted this. "We don't live in Boston." I didn't even know if I wanted to. *You know where you could live. You found the perfect place, too.* I shook the random thought aside, refusing to dig deep enough into it to make sense of it.

"I know there are details." She didn't sound deterred. "Money, moving… all that. But we're so close to a *yes* on the loan; I can feel it. We're right on that cusp, Andi. The property owner wants a tiny deposit. I have enough in savings to cover it. If I can do that, they'll hold the place for a month."

"A month is nothing." I should tell her *no*, but my doubt nagged. There was a reason property hunting was her job. She had an eye for these things, and I trusted her.

"This is a once-in-a-lifetime offer. We have to do this."

"I—" I couldn't refuse her "I have to get to the competition. Let me think about it for a day."

"All right. Twenty-four hours. And then I'll call them and tell them we'll get it."

"I'll talk to you tomorrow." Every inch of me tensed, muscles tightening to the point it ached. I clenched my teeth.

I got back to the table just as the waitress set our food down. I looked between the omelet in front of me and the guys.

Isaiah shrugged and gave me a tiny smile. "We have to be in the competition hall in less than an hour. You need food, to make your brain work."

"You expended a lot of energy yesterday." Kane topped off my coffee from the carafe the waitress left on the table.

Salsa covered the dish, and when I pressed my fork into the eggs, cheese melted out. From the brief glance I'd had at the menu, I didn't think this was an option, but it was exactly what I would have ordered. The gesture helped soothe my prickly nerves more than I thought possible, and I felt some of the stress drain from my neck. "Thanks."

"Marathon rounds today." Isaiah dropped the schedule on the table between us all. "You sure your fingers are up for this?" He winked at me.

I could handle this kind of teasing. It didn't make me wonder what came next. Instead it reinforced I wasn't the only one with pleasant memories. I waggled my fingers in the air. "They're feeling pretty limber. I'm good."

"And no holding back in anticipation of your plans tonight." Kane's tone was flat.

I jerked my head in his direction, and the spring that had been loosening inside me coiled to maximum capacity when he stared back, expression blank. "I'll mange both just fine." My words were clipped.

A tightrope of tension stretched between us. I pursed my lips, and he clenched his jaw.

"Less than an hour." Isaiah's kind warning broke the glaring match but didn't ease the churning inside me.

Conversation was stilted for the rest of breakfast, and I spent most of the meal watching my food. I wanted to ask Kane what was going on, but familiar doubt filled me. I had to be the one who didn't get it. If it were more, he'd say so. I didn't trust myself enough to believe otherwise.

We headed upstairs long enough to grab our gear for the next round. Most of our exchange consisted of nods, frowns, and single-syllable responses. I thought everything would be okay. They seemed so certain. It was all fun and games and incredible sex—and sure my heart felt like it might split at the notion our physical connection was only temporary, but that was on me.

Another thought joined the jumble. Was I about to do this to Glen?

Yeah, James was an asshole. I'd made a mistake with him. But was I really going to take that out on a random stranger? I leaned against a nearby wall, as the onslaught of uncertainty threatened to overwhelm me. A bubble swelled inside, filling my lungs. My stomach. My limbs. I tilted my head back and stared the ceiling, needing the blankness as a contrast to what I felt.

"Dee?" Isaiah's concern seeped through my confusion.

I sucked in a deep breath through my teeth and tried to force it into my veins. Two more times, and I found my voice. "I'm fine. I just need a minute. I'll catch up."

Kane moved into my line of sight. He tucked a strand of hair behind my ear, and I swore my chest was going to burst at the tentative touch. "We'll see you downstairs." The animosity had vanished from his words.

"Yeah." I stood there a little longer, trying to count off seconds rather than linger on confusion. I reached the point where I needed to hurry, or I'd miss competition check-in. The only thing I'd concluded, in a quagmire of uncertainty, was that I couldn't lead Glen on. He might not have a problem with it, or even react this way—maybe I was abnormal for letting this twist me in knots—but he didn't deserve to be an unwitting participant, and I didn't have the desire to explain the entire grudge-fuck thing to him, in order to make sure he was okay with it.

The room was empty when I reached it. I must have fallen into my head for longer than I thought. I grabbed my computer equipment and hurried back down to the competition hall. The clock ticked down. I scanned the crowds for my friends, and found them near the front entrance. My gaze drifted past Glen. He gave me a huge smile and waved. I really needed to tell him now that I couldn't meet up tonight, but I was relived there was no time. I returned the greeting, and then headed for Kane and Isaiah.

Isaiah rested a hand at the small of my back. "Better?" he asked.

I tried to look confident when I said, "Completely."

I was wrong. We settled in to game. The competition worked differently today. Every team had a set number of lives for each member and went one-on-one with another group. Once one set used their lives, the threesome still standing moved to the next still-standing block. Out of the remaining two hundred, the last fifty teams alive, would do the same thing this afternoon, with refreshed stats, until only eight were left.

We didn't fare well. From the moment they kicked off the start bell, I felt out of sorts with my friends. Barked commands held an edge that aggravated me. Each time I second-guessed their movements, I was wrong. Kane took a defensive position instead of pulling lead and going aggressive. None of it was right.

A counter rested in the upper right corner of our screens, ticking down as each group dropped out. When it hit sixty, Kane and I only had one life each, and Isaiah was at two. By fifty five, Isaiah had lost the extra.

I tried to keep my attention on the game, as the counter dropped toward fifty, but my focus was already fractured. I gripped my mouse so hard my fingers ached, and stars danced in front of my watering eyes as I strained to watch the screen.

"*Fuck*," Kane shouted in my headset. Seconds later, my own monitor exploded in a shower of red, indicating I'd been shot. The ticker hovered at fifty one.

"*Shit*," Isaiah yelled, and the ticker dropped to forty-nine.

Chapter Thirteen

The round was over, and the judges needed to make a call about who lost all their lives first. When I twitched my fingers against my leg, Isaiah covered my hand. I gave him a weak smile, but I didn't feel it.

They flashed our names up on the winners board, fiftieth place and moving on. We should be celebrating. Whooping and hollering like last night. The best we managed was a round of half-hearted hugs and high-fives. They called a thirty-minute intermission, for everyone going to the next round to rest their eyes and stretch their legs.

"Quick snack?" Isaiah tugged on my hand, to draw my attention.

I couldn't look at him. "I need to do... some stuff. I'll grab something and meet you back here."

Kane shouldered past us without a word.

"All right." Isaiah sounded as if it was

anything but. "Text me—us—if you change your mind."

"Sure." I needed some air and to be away from all these people. I cut a straight line to the nearest exit and pushed outside. I closed my eyes in the bright light and turned my face toward the sun. The heat didn't chase away the chill running under my skin, or the unshakable idea I wasn't the only one fumbling and lost. I couldn't do this. If the people around me struggled for answers, and I didn't have them…

I breathed in car exhaust and the sweltering summer. I'd already figured out one solution—how to deal with Glen—and I just needed to do it. Maybe I'd see if I could find him, and track down Isaiah and Kane after all. My stomach growled. Yeah, a snack before the next round was a good idea.

I pulled my phone out as I made my way back inside. I got full bars in the competition room, but my text to Isaiah failed to go through. The number of glows illuminating pale faces had to be causing too much interference. I dragged my feet back toward the casino.

Dante Larson, the chef we'd overheard last night, brushed past me. "Excuse me." His tone was gruff.

Go after him. There wasn't time now. Not that I had the guts anyway, but the no-time excuse sounded better in my head.

My step faltered, and my phone hand fell to my side. I barely had the presence of mind not to drop the device. Across the way, tucked back in a corner and almost hidden by slot machines, was

Isaiah, head bowed close to Glen's. Glen smiled, and then laughed. Isaiah said something else and shook his head. From where I stood, it looked as if they were both enjoying themselves.

What the fuck? I turned away, frustration clawing at my throat. I hadn't actually witnessed Isaiah flirting with the guy he encouraged me to hit on. I just had to ask Isaiah what they were talking about. It was time to stop worrying they might think my questions were stupid. I needed clarification, or I'd go insane balancing their friendship with my second-guessing.

"Andi, hi." Glen stepped in front of me, but he wouldn't meet my gaze.

I could ask him what they'd talked about, but that didn't feel right. The conversation I needed to have with Isaiah ran deeper than that curiosity. I did need to break off our date, though. "Hey. I'm glad you're here."

"Look, about later." He watched his feet, as he shifted his weight from one to the other. "I can't. This thing came up. Your friend. He... I have to— I'm sorry." He shoved something toward me, and I realized it was my USB cable. "Good luck." He turned away before he finished speaking, and was gone before I opened my mouth to reply.

Anger and hurt boiled inside, obliterating all of the positive feelings I had moments ago. I clenched my teeth so hard my jaw ached. Had Isaiah actually been flirting with him? Did he go behind my back and interfere, despite all the pushing he and Kane had done to get me to that point? Either way, I wanted answers.

I paced the short length of floor near the doors, trying to bring my emotions under control. The part of me that hated confrontation and preferred to let other people make the decisions wanted me to swallow these feelings. Stow them, paste on a smile until I believed myself, and go back in that room to win with my friends. Or at least, make it to the final eight.

"Players, the next round begins in two minutes."

The voice over the loudspeaker bounced in my head. Shit. I didn't realize I'd been out here so long. How had I missed the ten- and five-minute warnings?

I shoved my frustrations deep down inside and made my way back to our station. The room wasn't crowded the same way. Now most people sat in rows, watching the large screens at the front of the auditorium. There was more room at each table. Space to breathe. We'd made it this far; we could push to the next round.

The moment I saw Isaiah, my resolve poofed, and I stalked toward him. "What the hell did you say to him?"

"Dee." He grabbed my wrist loosely. "It wasn't—"

"Thirty seconds." The announcer's voice drowned out all chatter in the room, loud enough my ears rang even after he stopped talking.

Isaiah let go of me, but he didn't drop my gaze. "I'll explain."

"Save it." I fell into my seat, jammed on my headphones, and tried to find the right frame of mind just as the game kicked off.

My focus was anywhere but on the match. Everything any of us said was clipped and gruff. I couldn't find the pistol I wanted, Kane charged into the middle of ambushes again and again, and Isaiah missed half the shots he took with the sniper rifle.

Our lives ticked away as quickly as our ammo. The fifty-team count dropped to forty-five, and then forty. As my screen turned red, taking my last life with it, the competition counter hit thirty-nine. We were out.

"*Shit.*" Kane ripped off his headset and flung it across the table.

I rubbed my face, trying to scrub away the tension, but it didn't matter. Disappointment welled inside, carried on the knowledge we could have done better. That whatever fucked with our heads right now cost us this competition. Worse, it may have cost us something far more important. I clenched my fist until my nails dug into my palm. My thoughts echoed Kane's shout.

Chapter Fourteen

I jammed my gear into its bag. I should be crying, right? Sobbing with tears of disappointment? The feeling wasn't there. Around us, as more people were eliminated, it was the same. Instead of the fanfare of winning—the glee of going to the next round—the losers like us packed up their equipment. It was over, and I couldn't bring myself to pour any more emotion into the loss.

I whirled on Isaiah. "What did you say to him?"

He exhaled through his teeth and furrowed his brow. "I'm sorry. I... It was your choice to make. I shouldn't have taken it from you."

"Isaiah." I snipped off his name. "Tell me."

"That's what I did. I told him." Isaiah shouldered his laptop bag, blue eyes peering into my soul, searching for something I didn't think he'd find. "That you were coming down from a breakup. That the last guy cheated on you. That he should be careful how he handled you."

The confession didn't provide me the satisfaction I hoped for. It should have given me a reason to be furious or to hate him or to be able to walk away. "You're right. That was my call to make, not yours." My retort lacked passion.

"Sorry you missed out on your grudge fuck." Kane didn't project any of the sympathy or regret Isaiah did.

"Bullshit, you are." I glared at Kane. "I don't know what your issue is. Before now, this all went exactly the way you said you wanted. Except I don't know if that's true. You're pushing me with all this ask-if-you-want-it crap, and I can't get a solid read on you to save my sanity."

"So just—"

I held up my hand. "I swear to all that's holy, if you tell me to *just ask*, things will never be the same between us again."

"Because we have any chance of going back to that?" His question was bitter.

"Good point." I hated hearing him say it as much as I loathed that I couldn't argue. "I'm out of here." I whirled toward the exit. Walking away from them hurt far worse than losing the competition had. Ached more than finding James fucking another woman. Dug deeper than any disappointment I'd felt in a long time.

I didn't know where I was going, as I stepped from the casino. To another hotel room? That felt a little ridiculous. It certainly didn't tie into my realization I needed to talk to Isaiah and Kane, to twist my head on straight. Then again, I wasn't the only one who'd been holding back. Could I blame them? Sure, they'd peddled this stupid say-what's-on-your-mind spiel without meaning it themselves. It was sound advice, though, regardless of whether or not they believed it.

I wanted to go back and scream and yell, and make things right with them, but it wouldn't do me any good. There was no way to fix this. Kane had that right. I'd gotten sucked into a fantasy that wasn't mine.

And then I found a target for the disaster that was my mental state. James stood in the taxi line, staring off at nothing. Or maybe at the cute blond bending over to tuck something in her luggage.

"You stayed this long?" I asked, to get his attention.

He whirled, eyes wide, and then a smile spread over his face. "Andr— Andi. I wanted to see you compete. You did well."

"We sucked. We haven't played that poorly in ages." It felt good to admit it. Cleansing.

"Nah. You're being hard on yourself." He reached for me, and I stepped back. He frowned. "I'm sorry about everything. Have dinner with me. Let me explain."

Instinct wanted me to say, *all right*. Even if I had no intention of forgiving him, he might surprise me. He obviously thought he had something worth telling me. Who was I to argue? "No."

"Andrea."

A bitter laugh escaped my lips. "Why does it

even matter? Why try so hard to convince me we need another chance, when you were the one cheating on me?"

"Are you serious? Have you ever even been a part of this relationship?"

I snapped my jaw shut before it could drop open. "You're going to ask me that after months of rolling over and ignoring me in bed?"

"What was I going to do? Compete for your attention with those jackasses you call *gaming buddies*? Why even go out with me, if you already hooked up with them? Which one of them are you fucking? I'm guessing the blond one. "

The barrage of questions knocked my anger off balance, but I recovered quickly. "They're *friends*. Guess what, asshole. Guys and girls can be friends without it being about sex. Apparently, after my time with you, guys and girls can even date without it being about sex. I *never* cheated on you."

"The first thing you did was run into his arms." James was yelling now, and people stared.

I should have. The thought came from nowhere and settled in, feeling comfortable amid the tension. "If you weren't happy, why didn't you just break up with me?"

His upper lip pulled into a sneer. "That's what you ask. You don't want to know why I didn't talk to you, or why we couldn't work it out. Were you *ever* happy with me?"

The question sucked the venom from my retort, mingling with similar thoughts I'd had for the last few days. I believed I was. James said we were good together; I figured he saw something I didn't.

93

He said he loved me; I assumed he knew what he was talking about. When he suggested we move in together, my mind said, *why the hell not*. I shook my head. "No. I wasn't."

He stepped back from me. "Then I don't know why I stayed this long."

Was it really all my fault? I'd gone into this relationship under false pretenses. Led James on. Made him believe I felt something I didn't. Except at the time, I was sure my feelings were real.

"Goodbye, Andrea."

It was that name. It dug under my skin, and burrowed into my thoughts. Sparked already swelling irritation. He'd never gotten my name right. When I was annoyed, he managed to remember for a minute or two that I hated my full name. The rest of the time, no matter how many times I reminded him, he insisted *Andrea* was pretty, so that was what he'd call me.

That wasn't the only thing though. Insisting on ordering peppers on the entire pizza, even though I hated them. *Accidentally* throwing out frosting samples Julie made me, to make sure I could paint on them.

Mixed with the wash of realization was every kind gesture Isaiah and Kane had made without hesitation since they picked me up in Omaha. Even before then. They knew more about me than James ever bothered to learn, and I'd never met them in person until a few days ago.

I gave James my sweetest smile and let sugar spill into my voice. "Goodbye, James. I'll be by to get my stuff when you're not home. I'll leave my key on the table."

"You can't—"

"And I never want to see you again. We're done. It's over."

"You're not going to at least try to fix things?"

I stared at him in disbelief. "There's nothing to fix. We've always been broken. You don't fucking respect me. You never have. I don't know why you're still talking to me. Ego? You need someone to help pay the rent? It doesn't matter. This conversation is over, and so are we."

Chapter Fifteen

Are you upstairs? I sent the text to Isaiah and Kane. It was a relief to watch James ride off in a cab. He took more baggage with him than I realized I was carrying. Kane was right that we couldn't go back to what we had before, and maybe they didn't want me to be a part of their life in an intimate way, but I had to tell them how I felt. It might be a selfish decision, but I was tired of letting other people make up my mind for me.

Yes. Isaiah's message buzzed through. *You coming up?*

Yes. I wouldn't say more until we were face to face. I didn't want any room for misinterpretation.

Moments later, I slid the key into the hotel-room lock. The door jerked open, the handle pulling from my grasp and startling me. Isaiah met me. He studied me, and then grasped my face between his hands. When he crushed his mouth to mine, a whimper escaped my chest. My head swam, and I wanted to sink into the gesture. It would be so easy to just enjoy this kiss—the way his thumbs traced my cheekbones, his tongue dancing with mine, his teeth catching my lip when he broke away.

This had the potential to hurt, but it was better than pretending. "Stop," I forced myself to say. I struggled to catch my breath. "I can't... I mean, I can—I really want to—but I can't."

Isaiah trailed his palms down my arms, to grasp my fingers, and tugged me the rest of the way into the room. Kane stood behind him, arms crossed, watching us. I couldn't read his expression, and that strengthened my resolve even more.

I looked at Isaiah. "I know you're a touchy-feely person. Hugs, and this." I held our hands up. "But I can't take things to the level we have. Not in person. Making this friends-with-benefits relationship physical, bringing it into the real world, is more than I'm equipped for. So I'm sorry, but we need to dial this back."

I don't know what I expected Isaiah to do, but it wasn't to look over his shoulder at Kane, then back at me with a smile. "I'm not a touchy-feely person." He stroked his thumb over the back of my knuckles. "And honestly, this is wearing on me. I only act like this with him"—he jerked his head toward Kane—"and you."

"No, no, no." I couldn't hear this. It wasn't helping. I wanted his words to mean something, but without confirmation, they didn't. "You can't do that. You can't just spit these things out, wrapped in the just-friends excuse we've always clung to. I need you to spell this out for me. Here. I'll start." I faltered, the confession freezing in my throat. I swallowed hard to dislodge it. "I don't know how long I've felt this way, but here with you... I love you." It was terrifying and a relief to hear my own voice say that. "Both of you. And I know you were together before I came along, and you probably didn't go into this expecting me to feel this way, and I'm sorry if I took things wrong, but I—"

Isaiah kissed me again and swallowed my rambles. He let go of me and stepped back. "Expecting it? No. Not really. Hoping?" He moved aside and pointed me toward Kane. "I'm not doing this anymore."

At first I thought Isaiah was still talking to me, even as my mind tripped over what he meant. Then Kane looked past me, and I realized he was Isaiah's target.

Isaiah stood close enough to me that his heat radiated into my back. His voice was calm and even. "This is getting old, and it's going to break us. We've already started to fall apart. We should have made it further, down there. I'm not saying that because it matters we lost. This competition was a whim. We all knew that. The reason I care is because we click better than that, and something has fucked us up. Tell her, or you and I may start to fall apart too."

I heard the catch in Isaiah's voice at the same time Kane cringed. "No," I said quickly. "I don't want to come between you. That's not my point. God, that's the last thing I want."

Kane shook his head and strode toward me.

"You're not." He clenched his jaw, and seconds of silence stretched between us. "I asked him not to tell you. I didn't want to force it on you, if you didn't want it." His voice grew in volume. "We've been falling for you for ages. Not two days or the last couple of months, but since we started talking. Why the fuck do you think we flirt with you? And then you hooked up with that dickwad James. That tiny-pricked douche. And I swear, if he'd caused you more pain than a hangover, I would have laid him out. I wanted to, anyway. And hell, Andi, we've been fucking for two days, and it still didn't seem to click with you."

The accusation snapped something inside me, but it was muddled by everything else he'd said. "You should have just told me. Instead of nudging and prodding, and then pushing me toward Glen because the guy wanted to borrow a cable."

"I shouldn't have done that." Kane let out a shaky breath. "It's easy to ask for a hookup, but the thought of losing you…"

I wanted to be touched and to swoon and to fall into the surge of joy in my chest. We weren't done yet, though. "You spent days convincing me I need to learn to ask for what I want. Nudging and nagging. And you couldn't tell me yourself you were interested."

"Not just interested." Isaiah's even tone was a soothing contrast to the rising tension the room. "We're in love with you, Dee. That's not an easy thing to say."

"I…" I looked between the two of them. "Both of you?"

Kane shrugged. "Both of us. We're not complete without you. Hell, we haven't picked anyone else up since we really got to know you. The stories we told you all happened before. We shared because it's hot to do so and know you're enjoying it too."

"It is pretty hot." I ducked my head, but I was smiling. "You still should have told me."

Kane tangled his fingers in my hair and locked his gaze on mine. "I'm telling you now. *We're* telling you. I love you, Andi. More than anything or anyone except Isaiah, and there's really no way to rank that; you both land at the top of my list together. I know he feels the same." He kissed me, hard and hungry, devouring my words and making my heart soar.

I needed something to cling to, and dug my fingers into his arms. His muscles moved under my hands when he tightened his grip on me. This felt so right, I didn't know how I'd missed it before. How I let myself be convinced otherwise.

It didn't matter. We'd worked it out now, or at least took a really fantastic step in that direction. Isaiah brushed my hair aside and trailed his mouth along the back of my neck, and my heart threatened to burst from my chest. I wanted to lean back and forward at the same time, experience both touches and dive into everything at once.

I gasped when Kane pulled away. He kissed my cheek, down to my jaw, and along my throat. His mouth sent tremors through my skin when he spoke. "I'd never forgive myself if I drove you away." He kissed the hollow at the base of my throat, and then trailed along my collarbone. "I was an idiot. Isaiah tried to tell me, and I was stubborn." He followed a line down my chest with his mouth. "Let us make it up to you now."

I wanted to tease him. Ask how Isaiah had gotten sucked into Kane's apology. I liked the idea of them making things up to me too much to risk spoiling the mood. "Curious to see what you've got." My light laugh melted into a sigh when he nipped at my skin.

Chapter Sixteen

Isaiah rested his palms on my stomach, under my shirt. The heat of his touch was better than the morning sun on my face. He nuzzled my hair aside, then caught my earlobe in his teeth, before tugging and letting go. "So you like to watch?"

I liked a lot of things, some of them only fantasy—for now. Mostly I liked the idea of spending as much time as physically possibly with both of them, exploring and playing and touching. Though the thought lit up my nerve endings and made me tingle, it was a bit vague. "It's definitely a turn-on. Especially with you two."

Isaiah glided his hands to my breasts and teased through the fabric with a barely-there caress. "So when you're by yourself, do you trawl the internet for naughty pictures?"

"Pictures. Movies. Gifs." I groaned when he

brushed my nipples. "Anyone who looks like they're having fun."

"What if it went both ways?" Kane pulled my shirt over my head. "Like last night?"

I hadn't really thought about it before. The guys I'd dated didn't want to see me play with myself. Kane's question triggered a series of images and sensations. How much I loved his gaze on me, while Isaiah sucked him off. The way it intensified the moment. My already hard nipples strained to get closer to Isaiah's touch, and I felt myself grow wet at the thought. "I like the sound of that."

Disappointment filtered in when Isaiah's touch fell away, but it didn't last long. Kane kissed me hard again, crashing against mouth. His frame rubbed against mine, but it wasn't enough. I wanted to feel everything. I tugged at the hem of his shirt, and he broke away long enough to strip it off, before diving back into me. I shifted my weight, unable to ignore the pulse of want below my waist, but adjusting myself so the seam of my jeans rubbed my clit didn't provide the relief I wanted.

I dropped my hand to Kane's crotch and traced his erection through the fabric. He hissed and thrust against my palm. His grip on me shifted, and I thought he was going to help me strip off the rest of our clothes. A new bolt of shock and want raced through me when he grabbed one wrist, circled me, and pulled my other arm behind my back as well.

"You're moving too fast." His warning teased my skin. He wrapped something soft but taut—a T-shirt maybe—around my arms, just below the elbows, and wrapped it a couple more times until it ended at my wrists, binding me. I tugged enough to know he wanted me to stay put, but I didn't try to break free. The loss of movement, the surrender of my mobility to him, was both terrifying and squirm-worthy.

The sound of a zipper drew my attention. Isaiah stood several feet back, in front of an armchair, stripping off his clothes. Shirt first—and God, I still liked seeing his bare chest. I itched to trace the definition. To dig my fingers into the firm muscle.

Kane snaked a hand up my stomach and pushed my bra out of the way, rough elastic scraping its way up and heightening my senses. "Take the time to enjoy this." He kissed along my shoulder, and feathered touches over my nipples so lightly, I wasn't sure if I wanted to moan or giggle.

Isaiah kicked off his shoes and socks, then pushed his jeans and boxers to the ground. His cock sprung free, standing at attention. I wanted to wrap my fingers around it. Lick the head. Suck on him, until he was so close he could barely hold back, and then feel him drive inside me.

But a show might be just as good. He dropped into the chair and took his shaft in his hand. As he stroked, he watched me, blue eyes hooded and dark. Kane pinched one nipple, and I groaned in surprise.

"More." My voice came out a dry rasp.

Kane's chuckle filled my head and flustered my thoughts. He tweaked harder, rolling the nub between his fingers, pulling and stretching. The throbbing ache between my thighs grew, as I sank into the feeling and watched Isaiah's hand glide up and down at a steady pace.

I pushed my ass back into Kane, trying to grind against him, but he stood just out of reach. "Do you want me to untie you?" he asked. "I'll do it now, and you can dictate exactly how fast this ends. Or, if you trust me…"

As much as I ached to feel him push between my legs—to be stretched out and fucked right now—I had a feeling the wait would be worth it. "I trust you. Always." The words meant far more than I intended them to. I didn't know if he heard the catch in my voice, but I realized I was willing to put all my faith in these two, because they did the same with me.

"Glad to hear it." He gripped my chin and locked my head in a position to watch Isaiah. "Don't look away."

I was searching for a witty version of *I wasn't planning on it*, when Kane shoved his hand past my waistband. The rough denim pressed against my skin, drawing tighter as he dipped his fingers between my legs. I gasped when he brushed my slit and slipped easily along the path.

"When you told us how wet you got"—he dipped near my opening and back toward my clit, but never touched either one—"I thought it was just internet dirty talk." He slid inside me just enough to tease, before gliding back up again. "But fuck, you're soaked. I want to feel you wrapped around me soon."

Each time he drew close to my swollen button, I whimpered and tried to push nearer to his touch. The way he held me made it difficult, but the response was instinct. Isaiah watched us through half-closed eyes, his speed increasing with each desperate sound I made. Geez, that was sexy, watching him masturbate because of us. Losing myself in Kane's touch and at the same time imagining it was me, stroking Isaiah's cock.

"When you finish yourself off, do you drag it out, or make it fast?"

Embarrassment raced through me, mingling with everything else and making me hyper aware of his touch. "It's always fast. So no one hears." I wasn't ashamed of it, but I hated that I'd put myself in relationships where finishing myself off quickly and quietly became status quo.

"That's too bad." He brushed my clit, and a cry tore from my throat. "I love the sounds you make when you're turned on. I want more."

"That makes two of us," I managed, before he honed in on my sex again.

Already lost in everything surrounding us, I was so close to climax, I almost came when he lingered for more than a second. He eased off again when my gasps became shorter and my voice louder.

Isaiah clenched his jaw. He was getting close as well. I could see it in the heave of his chest. Hear it in his grunts. His gaze never left me. "My second favorite sound in the world is you, coming. It's even better in person." His words were labored, punctuated with grunts as he stroked himself faster.

"First favorite?" My question faded into another strangled cry when Kane lingered on my clit longer. Waves of pleasure lapped at my senses.

"Hearing both you and Isaiah at the same time." Kane wrapped his fingers around my button, never letting my attention stray from Isaiah's face, holding me captive with bound arms and still-fastened jeans. He rubbed hard and fast, easing off for only a second, each time my cries grew louder. He finally applied more pressure, drawing out my climax, stroking me until I screamed and my pussy clenched and my legs wobbled. He held me upright, not easing off. Isaiah leaned his head back with a groan and bucked against his touch, his cum shooting out and covering his own hand.

It wasn't until he shuddered and stopped, that Kane eased off. He let go of my chin and dropped his hand to my stomach, pulled me back into his chest, and held me. His kisses were tender and alluring against the bare skin of my shoulder.

The tension in my neck eased when he finally undid my bindings. I rolled my shoulders, to get sensation back. I pulled his hand from my pants and raised his fingers to my lips, to suck him clean one digit at a time. He moaned, his erection digging into my ass and teasing me each time I flicked my tongue over another pad.

Isaiah grabbed a handful of tissue from the nightstand and cleaned himself up.

"Worth it?" Kane moved his lips along my bare back, right below my neck.

"God, yes." I was finally catching my breath.

"I meant what I said earlier." He undid the button on my jeans and dragged down the zipper. "I want to feel you wrapped around my cock."

Chapter Seventeen

Kane helped me balance long enough to toe off my sneakers, then scraped the rest of my clothing down my legs. I heard the rapid click of a zipper, and what sounded like foil tearing. Hand on the small of my back, he pushed me forward. I caught myself on the bed, weight resting on my palms. He grabbed my hips and urged me forward, until I knelt on the mattress on all fours.

"Gorgeous ass." He caressed the curve, before slapping it hard enough to sting.

I bit my lip but couldn't hold back my whimper of pleasure.

"Sexy voice." He shoved two fingers inside me, spreading me open and making me arch my back. "Tight, wet pussy." He grabbed my hair, pulled my head back, and bent enough to kiss me. "Amazing mind." He pulled his fingers out of me.

"Absolutely perfect."

He let go of my head and grabbed my hip. With no other warning, he plunged his cock deep inside me, stretching and filling me. I thought I was spent, but each new thrust drew me back into the sensations a little more. The mattress shifted, almost throwing me off balance, but Kane didn't let up on the steady, deep pounding. He grabbed my throat and pulled me half upright. His fingers gripped tight enough I couldn't ignore the possession, but not so much I wanted to pull away.

Isaiah knelt in front of me. He nibbled at my bottom lip, then traced his tongue along the tender skin, before pressing his mouth to mine. It was enough to steal my breath, and Kane's grip kept me from completely finding it again. It was the right amount of pressure on my windpipe for my thoughts to float in a pleasant cloud. Kane dug into my hip with his other hand, slamming inside me harder the more Isaiah deepened the kiss. My whimpers were weak, vanishing into his mouth.

Each time Kane drove deeper, he struck a spot that flared with intense pleasure, bordering on the edge of uncomfortable and incredible.

Isaiah pushed me upright more. Black spots hovered at the edge of my vision, dancing in time with the demanding pace Kane set. When Isaiah dropped his hand between my thighs to stroke my still-tender clit, I clenched tight around Kane's cock. Instinct told me to pull away, but even if they didn't have me trapped, I wanted to ride this out. Kane tightened his grip on my throat, but not enough to limit my breathing further.

"Fuck, Andi." His words were jagged, tearing with each new push inside me. "The fantasy was never this good. Not even close."

Even if my mouth weren't otherwise occupied, I wouldn't have the brainpower to reply. Isaiah stroked my clit hard and fast, pushing me past *too much*. The stimulation mingled with Kane's movement, filling my thoughts and forcing climax over me, until it rolled through every inch of my body. I had to break away from Isaiah's kiss and draw in more air, to scream in pleasure when I came. And still they didn't let up.

Kane squeezed my hip tighter, as his thrusts grew frantic and shallow. He grunted and slammed his pelvis against my ass, until he let out a drawn out groan of orgasm, and slowed to a stop.

He eased out of me, then collapsed on the bed and pulled me back into him. My legs were grateful for the relief, and my throat and lungs burned with the rush of oxygen. I couldn't focus on anything besides the comfort of his arm around me.

Isaiah lay in front of me. He rested his hand on the back of my neck and pressed his forehead to mine. "We're so lucky you're here."

I smiled and closed my eyes, feeling more relaxed than I had in days. "Me too. I mean…"

Kane laughed and gave me a light squeeze. "We get it."

****

We were up half the night, laughing, talking, not gaming, and only getting dressed when Kane

110

ordered dinner and had to answer the door.

The next morning, Isaiah almost proved all three of us could fit in the shower, but no one really got clean. After a few minutes of giggling and groping, I reluctantly convinced him it wasn't going to happen. At least not in this shower, if we intended to do more than feel each other up.

If we'd made it to the competition finals, we would have been expected downstairs early, for a grueling match meant to test the mettle of the final eight. Instead, we took our time with breakfast and trying to decide what we wanted to do with our last free day, before we had to go home.

None of us had figured out a solution to that yet. I didn't have a place to live when I got back, but it wasn't as if I could pick up and move to Chicago. Until I got financing for the cookies, I had to keep my day job.

"We'll hook up on long weekends," Isaiah promised. "And you're never more than a message away."

"I know. But it's not the same." I was trying to keep a positive outlook, but it bummed me out to have to put that much distance between us so soon. My phone chimed, cutting into the conversation. It was Julie.

Crap, I was supposed to call her back this morning. I gave the guys an apologetic smile, and answered. "I'm so sorry."

"Don't. I'm never, ever letting you go on vacation with those guys again, if it means you keep forgetting about me." Her voice was loud enough I had to hold the receiver away from my ear.

Kane and Isaiah both watched me with raised brows and curious amusement. Julie didn't sound pissed though, so much as high strung and frustrated.

"I really am sorry. I…" I was going to have to explain all of this to her. That might take some time. I might convince the guys to stop in Omaha long enough to meet her and show her internet people were, in fact, real. Images of the last few days flashed through my mind, vivid and graphic and complete with sensory input, and heat filled me. Some more real than others. That wasn't why she called though, and taking care of business was important. "The answer is no," I said.

"Andi." A hint of pleading leaked into her voice. "Downtown, historical Boston. We aren't going to find another opportunity this incredible, especially if we want a storefront in a big city."

"I know, but I can't do this deal." Indecision warred inside, and looking at the two people watching me, trying to decipher details based on half a conversation, didn't help. What if Julie was right? Could we afford to pass up something like this? I met Kane's gaze, and inspiration—insane, impulsive, and possibly stupid inspiration—flared inside me. "What about Chicago?"

Kane leaned forward, lips twitching in an unformed smile.

Julie's laugh stretched on for several seconds. "Sorry. You're serious. We're not going to find rent this cheap back home, let alone someplace like Chicago."

"But what if we could?"

"I'd go in a heartbeat. But just because your

internet friends live there doesn't mean we should set unrealistic goals."

We definitely needed to have a talk about that. "Hang on." I pulled the receiver from my mouth enough I wouldn't talk into her ear, but not so much she couldn't hear me. I looked at Kane. "That property you can't rent. What are the odds you could hold it for a month, if we put a deposit on it?"

He broke into a grin. "I'll make it happen."

I switched back to Julie. "Did you hear that?"

"There's no way he can match the Boston deal." Despite Julie's words, I'd known her long enough to recognize the hope in her voice. "Can he? Does this mean we're finally pulling the trigger, instead of dancing around the financing excuse?"

"It's not an excuse, but we'll find the money. And yeah, even with the rose-colored lenses off, this place is nicer than the one you found. Rent's a teensy bit higher, but I understand the landlord is motivated."

"*Yes.*" Julie's shout made my eardrum ring. "This is important, so don't forget this time. Get me a final amount as soon as you have it, of how much you need from me, for the deposit."

"I will. I promise. Talk soon?"

"Damn straight."

I hung up and dropped my phone back in my purse.

"Are you kidding me?" Isaiah looked like he could barely sit still. "You're going to move to Chicago?"

"The place has an apartment upstairs." I had to be smiling like an insane person. "I have to work the numbers, and in the long run, we still need a loan, but if all the money I'd spend on rent is going into the place, and I split that with Julie—"

Kane stood, leaned across the table, and kissed me hard. "You'll have a lease on Monday. Deposit to hold it for a month, so you can make sure. I'll make it work for you."

An unshakable giddiness floated through me, as we paid for breakfast and made our way back toward the hotel casino, trying to decide what to do next, but continuously getting distracted by the very real possibility of me moving closer to them.

I stalled, feet freezing in place and plans evaporating, when I saw Dante Larson walking toward the front exit, luggage in tow.

"Dee?" Isaiah said.

I held up my index finger and spoke before my brain could catch up and talk me out of it. "I'll be right back." I sprinted toward the exit. "Excuse me, Mister Larson."

His shoulders rose and fell in an exaggerated movement, before he turned to face me, scowl etched on his face. "I don't have time for pictures or ramblings or stories about how much your grandmother loves me. I have a plane to catch."

The abrupt response grated on me, but it didn't deter me. Up close, I realized he was actually as attractive as on TV, and probably no older than I was. How odd would that be, to have accomplished so much before thirty? And to still be an ass on top of it all?

"I only need two minutes. Less time than it will take for you to talk me out of it. I have a business proposal for you."

"Auditions ended yesterday. You should have gone through proper channels." He back toward the exit.

"I know, but I—" I clipped off what was about to be a rambling apology when I realized he was almost out of hearing range. Fuck it. Now or never, right? "Hand-painted video-game characters bouquets on the best fucking cookies you've ever tasted." Maybe I shouldn't have sworn as part of my pitch, but he was walking away either way.

He paused and turned. "Are the designs any good?"

I hesitated. Talking up Julie's baking was simple. Bragging about my own art was another matter entirely. Which might be part of what held me back. "They're brilliant. Gorgeous." It felt odd to talk about myself like that. But I had to sell it, right?

He glanced at his watch. "I have to go."

"Wait." I was ready to beg. "I have a full proposal. Business plan, profit and loss projections, a proven distribution model—all in writing."

He studied me for a moment and then took his wallet from his back pocket. He pulled out a business card and handed it to me. "Email me. Have it in my inbox by Monday morning. If it's as good as you say, we'll talk."

"Thank you." I wanted to jump up and down but settled for taking his card.

"No promises. I just said we'd talk."

"That's all I ask."

He shook his head and turned away, picking up his pace as he headed for the cab line.

Kane stepped up next to me and wrapped an arm around my waist. I leaned into him and tangled my fingers with Isaiah's. My chest felt like it might burst from all the fantastic *maybe*s. I was willing to pour everything I had into making this work. This relationship, this business—all of it.

And I was looking forward to doing it all with the people I loved.

Epilogue

I dropped another box in the corner of my new bedroom. At least for now. In the month since getting back home from Vegas, the long-distance conversations with Kane and Isaiah as well as the couple of weekend visits made me think I might be living with them soon. I turned back toward the stairs leading down to what would be the bakery and our new retail storefront. The stairwell emptied out between the two and led directly to the alley, so we could either turn into work or head straight for our cars out back.

Julie thought it would be odd having a roommate, but she'd been letting me crash in her spare room anyway, since it didn't make sense for me to rent another place after I got all my stuff from James's apartment. It took her some time to get used to my relationship with Kane and Isaiah. She said it wasn't because of the threesome, but because she still struggled to believe I'd found not one, but two nice guys online.

Instead of turning toward the cars when I got downstairs, I headed for the shop. Nervous, happy flutters spun in my gut. Giving my notice at work was only one of dozens of amazing occurrences the last few weeks. The place was ours. Dante Larson gave us enough money to pay our salaries and work within the business plan for the first year.

Well, *gave* wasn't the right word. And unlike a bank, this wasn't a loan. He was an investor, who had a say in this. The thought made me anxious, but it turned out when he wasn't grumpy and late for his plane, he wasn't a total asshole. Julie disagreed, but for the most part I kept the two of them away from each other.

Paper still lined the store windows. It would come down after we finished remodeling or got close enough to tease the outside world.

Someone leaned against the doorframe next to me, and I didn't have to look, to know it was Julie. Even if the faint jasmine perfume she always wore didn't give her away, her happy sigh would have. "We did it." Excitement filled her words.

I couldn't help my grin. "Not completely. But we're getting closer."

"Are you pleased with yourselves?" Isaiah wrapped his arms around my waist and kissed the top of my head.

"Absolutely." Julie and I spoke in unison, glanced at each other, and laughed.

I leaned back into Isaiah. This was so perfect.

Not that we didn't still have a ton to do, but this felt right.

"Am I the only one still working?" Kane's question didn't shatter the mood so much, as added a new level to it.

I turned to face him, and Isaiah kept one hand on my hip. I trailed my gaze over Kane. Tall, lanky, still gorgeous even with sweat hugging his T-shirt to his torso. I stepped closer. "You look sexy, working so hard. Doesn't that make it worth it?"

"No." He shook his head. "But seeing you smile does. Making you scream later doesn't hurt either."

Julie pushed away from the wall and headed toward the door. "Do that back at your place. And I don't want details," she called over her shoulder.

"That's not what you told me on the drive into town," I said, teasing in my voice.

Never looking back, she held her hand up over her shoulder, middle finger extended. "Tell the world, why don't you? You know I was kidding."

"I know." My exaggerated sigh ended in a laugh, and she disappeared around the corner.

"Good." Isaiah embraced me again. "That's between us."

Kane tilted my head up and kissed me. This was never getting old. We really had done it. Even though we weren't open for business yet, we were on our way. And I had the two most amazing men in the universe, supporting me for the adventure. Life was about to get interesting in the best way possible.

THE END

~*~

If you'd like to get to know Julie and Dante better, and meet Christopher, *Control Games* (Game for Cookies Book 2) keep reading for a free sneak preview of chapter one

~*~

Control Games

Chapter One

Julie nestled her last mixing bowl in its spot in the kitchen cabinet, then scanned the room one final time. Spotless. Perfect. Everything tucked away where she wanted it. And all before five. Over the past few months, she'd discovered the biggest problem with living above the bakery she owned with her best friend Andi was that, at the end of the day, it was harder to drag herself away and head home.

There was always just one more thing for Julie to do before she headed upstairs, to prep the place for its grand opening in two weeks. Always one more thing to do, to make sure everything was exactly the way she needed it to be.

"I've been thinking…" Dante interrupted her moment of quiet bliss.

And then there was this guy. She got the

eye-rolling out of her system before facing him, and squelched the desire to ask if the thinking hurt. She was trying to learn to play nice with him. Mostly because his financial investment and top-ranked TV cooking show were the reasons she and Andi could expand like this. At least a little because Andi insisted Dante was a nice guy and Julie needed to give him a chance.

She met his gaze. None of her decision to be kind had anything to do with the fact his spiky blond hair and piercing blue eyes stole her breath and sent vivid fantasies racing through her thoughts. Besides, Dante hadn't said anything wrong tonight. *Yet.* "Thinking what?" she asked.

"Chocolate and vanilla aren't enough. We need at least one more flavor."

Again she held her tongue kept Andi's advice in mind. If Julie wouldn't snap at someone she liked for saying the things Dante did, he was probably being reasonable. Once upon a time, she respected him. It wasn't just that he had a top-ranked cooking show. He'd taken his skill as a chef, turned it into a living, and used his fame and wealth to boost other businesses like hers and Andi's. He invested and helped them grow and become something.

Then Julie met the guy and discovered the asinine persona on the television translated to real life.

"In time for initial filming," he said before she could respond. "Unless you can't bake a couple cookies in three days."

And there it was—the hint of disdain. The implication she wasn't capable of doing her job. A twitch throbbed behind her right eye. The start of her next headache. "To whip up three thousand or so cookies? It's plenty of time." At least that many, in this amazing place. "To come up with a new recipe that meets my standards? Are you insane or just a sadist?"

He made a noise that fell somewhere between a sigh and a growl. "They're fucking cookies, and it's not like they need artwork. Not yet. I'm only asking they be available as samples, when the cameras roll. I'm thinking chocolate chip."

Her headache amped up another tick. "I know you're a busy guy, but if you're going to take part in these conversations and make these decisions, you need to listen when I tell you things like *we can't use drop cookies in our bouquets.* Or maybe you didn't hear me the first dozen times I said it." She and Andi had found their niche—custom-painted game-and-movie-characters on cookie bouquets. And unless they were making Jabba the Hut cookies, or his non-copyright-violating equivalent, Jebba the Gut, no blob-shaped cookie would fit the bill.

"Then make rolled cookies with chocolate chips in them. Outside the box, doll. That's your thing, right? I can't do all the thinking for you."

Julie clenched her fist, to keep from grabbing the rolling pin on the counter and throwing it at him. "We've got less than two weeks." She failed to keep the frustration from her voice. "Why did you wait to come to me with this?"

"I was hoping, with the right nudging—especially after the chocolate conversation—you'd come up with it on your own,

Ms.
I'm-a-Cordon-Bleu-Trained-Baker-who-doesn't-nee
d-input-from-anyone."

The snideness in his words pushed every last one of her buttons, and she gritted her teeth until her jaw ached. Being furious about his tone was easier than admitting it hurt that someone she used to respect didn't care for her skill. She forced out the words in a slow, even tone. "This is the kind of thing you don't hint at or leave until the last minute."

"You don't want help, then?"

"I've got it just fine—thank you very much." She didn't. She had no idea how she was going to pull this off. It wasn't that a new cookie recipe was a complex thing, but finding one that held up to the frosting Andi painted on, and tasted good and didn't crumble in transit... That was a different story.

No reason to let him know that. The night already promised to be long, with this latest information; she wasn't going to let his attitude add an extra kick of irritation.

So much for getting out of work on time.

* * * *

Dante intended to suggest the new flavor idea, apologize for not thinking of it sooner, and help Julie brainstorm a solution. He still could. Take Christopher's advice about trying to get along with her, apologize, and set this right.

But God fuck it, if she wasn't infuriating sometimes. Most of the time. She stretched his every last nerve along a tightrope and had the audacity to

124

look incredible and unapologetic in the process. Like now. Pink flushed her cheeks, and her lips were drawn into a thin line that made him want to kiss away her irritation until she was weak in the knees.

"Great. Glad it's under control." The words came out laced with more sarcasm than he intended. Her cringe was subtle. *Serves her right.* He didn't feel the venom he needed to believe the thought. "I'm out of here for the night. We'll pick it up in the morning."

She crossed her arms and stepped back. "*We* won't do anything. I've got this."

"Of course you do. Good night."

She probably flipped off his back as he walked out of the kitchen. He didn't care. He was focused on calming breaths. *Inhale deep, hold it, and exhale.* As a business idea, this setup was brilliant. Julie and Andi had the perfect combination of gimmick and quality with their product. As a business partner, Julie sent his blood pressure through the roof. Over and over and over. Stubborn, unyielding, and always needing things her way.

Not to mention gorgeous, intelligent, and quick-witted, but if he thought about her good points, he'd feel bad about the way he left things.

Dante climbed into his car and pointed toward the house he and Christopher had rented for the duration of their stay. Dante didn't know what was worse about Julie—her refusal to ask for help, or how gorgeous she looked, even angry. It wasn't that her rage made her more attractive. With deep brown eyes, dark hair, and the kind of gorgeous, full curves years of baking honed, she was striking enough her fury didn't detract from it.

She was also more stubborn than his ex-wife, and the last thing he needed was a temper to match his own. By contrast, another reason he loved Christopher was that he was Dante's pillar of sanity amid the chaos.

Dante navigated the traffic on auto-pilot. They'd been staying in Chicago for the last couple of months—plenty of time for him to familiarize himself with the layout. Besides, Christopher grew up here and had given Dante a fantastic tour from a local's point of view. They'd picked a place outside the metro area, in Schaumburg instead of downtown Chicago because Christopher insisted it was far enough to keep them sane when they wanted quiet, but close enough for them to still reasonably commute.

Dante hoped thoughts of his boyfriend—tall, dark haired, and better built than an I.T. guy had the right to be—would take his mind off the irritation Julie caused. Instead, they were a reminder of the tension at home. Never severe. Just the underlying hum that things weren't going well between Dante and his network; Christopher would rather see him walk away than put up with the shit.

The reminder led to Julie and Christopher becoming part of a single image in Dante's head. Some couples were driven apart by jealousy. However, while there was always a healthy whisper of doubt in the back of Dante's mind when he and Christopher brought a third into their playtime, for the most part he loved watching Christopher with someone else. Seeing the man he loved take control in the bedroom. Experiencing new kinks and desires with each new shared lover.

As frustrating as Julie was, Dante very much appreciated the fantasy of Christopher stripping her down, pinning her to the wall, and sliding inside her. Imagining her cries of pleasure as Christopher drove his thick cock deeper with each thrust. Her smooth, pale skin glistening with exertion.

Dante's dick hardened, straining against his jeans and demanding attention. He bit the inside of his cheek, to drag himself from the visuals and back to his commute. He couldn't rid his mind of the notion, and while he wished it starred someone other than her, that didn't stop the idea from sliding over every inch of his senses. By the time he pulled into the driveway, he itched to slide down his zipper and jerk off right there.

He had a better idea. One that would make the release that much sweeter and far better than taking matters into his own hands.

* * * *

Christopher leaned back in the kitchen chair and rubbed his eyes, to restore moisture. He didn't have to take a contract job during this trip; the fee he billed for installing the security cameras at L&D Cookies was better than his standard rate. But the work didn't take much time, and he could only play so many video games waiting for Dante to get back each day, before his mind numbed and he couldn't process basic language anymore.

It hadn't always been that way. Once upon a

time, he was more a part of Dante's creative process. They started this TV-chef thing as a team, and Christopher hated that Dante had drifted away from that part of their connection. So Christopher picked up spare contracts when he needed to pass the time.

The deadbolt on the front door thunked open, and Christopher couldn't help his smile when Dante walked into the house. *Speaking of...*

"Help me understand"—Dante's stripped off his shoes and shed his keys—"what it is you see in that woman?"

This must be about Julie. It usually was, these days. Creative, attractive, and the current bane of Dante's existence. Christopher would rather get to know every inch of her—remove her clothes a tantalizing piece at a time, see if she'd surrender her tight grasp on control once he had her naked—than listen to her argue with Dante. "What did she do now? Or rather, what do you *think* she did now?" Christopher asked.

"I don't know. *Blah, blah, blah. I'm right, and you're wrong. Blah, blah...*"

Christopher gave Dante his full attention.

"God, I'd like to watch you fuck her," Dante said, meeting his gaze, heat smoldering in his eyes.

"I never should have told you I thought she was attractive." Christopher didn't mean it. The confession slipped out one night, while he was trying to convince Dante to give the woman a break, but its being out there benefited Christopher as much as it was used against him. Dante's expression said this would be an instance of the former. "Besides, I don't think she's the type of woman who's going to let you

128

gag her, so you'd still have to hear her talk," Christopher said.

Dante closed the distance between them but stopped out of reach. "Your cock in her mouth would have a similar effect."

"You know you're a fucking asshole, don't you?" Teasing lined Christopher's words, but he was serious. Humiliation wasn't his kink. That didn't stop the thought of Julie's lips wrapped around his shaft from assaulting him. He imagined her dropping to her knees, taking him in her mouth, and groaning against his skin as she sucked.

"Call me all the names you want. You're picturing it."

"And?" Christopher recognized the playful jab in Dante's retort. The light-hearted tone. The fact none of it was meant to insult. This was much better than the arguments they'd had recently about Dante's job. That Christopher wasn't happy being left out of business decisions. That being relegated to IT guy not having a say in the show he and Dante created, was draining his brain. At least when they were fucking, that tension vanished in the background.

Dante leaned over, lips millimeters from Christopher's. "And your protests don't carry the same impact when you're already hard at the thought." Dante knelt, and dragged down the zipper on Christopher's jeans. When he worked Christopher's dick free, Christopher hissed at the contrast of a cool hand on his hot skin.

When they'd met, Dante would have been more likely to give up cooking than vocalize his desires. It was part of the reason Rachel and Dante sought out Christopher, in his old profession as a sex therapist. It took a little coaching, and a lot of incredible hands-on practice, and Dante developed a new comfort level with taking about his fantasies.

"It's all about consent." Christopher's voice wavered when Dante dragged a thumb over the head of his cock. "I'd enjoy it if she did." His playful retort faded into a groan.

Dante tightened his grip around Christopher's shaft, stroking at a steady pace. "I'm sure. Then, if you were there early one morning, and she didn't realize it, and wandered downstairs in just a T-shirt and panties, you'd wait for her to make the first move."

Christopher hissed at the combination of mental image and physical contact. "I don't like the idea of leaving that up to fate. I'd have to at least prompt her. Make sure she knew there were a lot of possibilities on the table. Or the counter. Or bent over the back of a chair."

"Especially with that gorgeous ass on display? Begging to be slapped?"

Flame seared across Christopher's skin at the idea. "Or sliding up behind her, dragging a finger along the elastic, and teasing her until she was soaked and begging for release."

"She argues someone could come in at any minute, and you ask if she wants you to stop. The shake of her head tells you all you need to know. You need to be inside her. She whimpers and says *yes, Sir.*"

Fantasy blurred with reality, merging at the

one point they had in common. Christopher wanted something more tactile and full-body. Need, dark and thick, pulsed inside him. He pulled Dante to his feet and knotted his fingers in Dante's hair. Christopher kissed him hard, crushing their mouths together until teeth cut into lips, swallowing Dante's groans.

He yanked Dante's head back to look him in the eye. "This isn't enough," Christopher growled.

Dante's smirk vanished behind wide-eyed desire. "Whatever you want."

"I'll figure that out as we go." Christopher pushed Dante toward the bedroom and the bed, making a quick stop at the dresser to grab the lube. He kissed along the back of Dante's neck, losing himself in the familiar scent of baked sugar mixed with faint cologne.

Dante's well-painted story was gone, replaced with groans. He leaned back into Christopher, head tilted to the side to receive more attention.

Christopher fisted his own cock, stroking slowly. He trailed his tongue along the edge of Dante's ear. "Pants off, and kneel on the mattress," Christopher said.

Dante nodded and complied. Christopher squeezed a dollop of lube into his hand, and glided his fingers along Dante's ass. Dante gasped at the first touch of room-temperature liquid. The sounded blended into a groan when Christopher teased his opening with slick fingers.

Christopher nudged Dante's entrance with the head of his cock, then penetrated him an inch at a time, sliding in at an excruciatingly slow pace. When he was buried to the hilt, he adopted an even rhythm, at a similar speed to the one Dante teased him with moments ago.

At the same time, he reached around and gripped Dante's shaft. Christopher accelerated his pumping, stroking Dante faster, squeezing enough it had to send a light ache through his lover. Dante moaned in response, fucking Christopher's fist.

Each time Dante's groans reached the familiar, fevered pitch of nearing climax, Christopher eased off. Dante thrust his hips to increase the attention again, but Christopher held back.

"Please." Dante's voice was low, a grumble rolling through it. "Let me come."

The appeal rolled over Christopher, singeing his skin and tightening in his balls. He sped up, pumping Dante hard, not easing up when he let out a throaty cry and climaxed, coating Christopher's hand with sticky fluid.

Christopher loosened his grip, but didn't let go, despite the occasional shudder racing through Dante. His dick had to be tender, and Christopher was enjoying the teasing. He thrust harder inside Dante, and was greeted with an arched back and a loud gasp.

He couldn't hold back anymore. He moved both hands to Dante's hips, squeezing tight as he pounded inside. Christopher's thoughts swam and flitted into oblivion, leaving pleasure in their wake. The edges of his vision blurred as he neared orgasm.

He came hard, thrusting until he was spent.

His breath tore from his lungs in jagged shards. Christopher leaned forward and lay a line of kisses along Dante's spine. "God, you tell a good story." Christopher gave a throaty chuckle.

"I've got an excellent muse." Dante moved forward and dropped to the bed as Christopher softened and pulled out of him.

They cleaned up, and climbed into bed next to each other, a light haze of bliss drifting through the room.

"Are you going to tell me what Julie did?" Christopher asked.

"Same shit, different day. And it's possible I provoked her a little bit."

"I can't imagine." It was a symptom of the rift growing between him and Dante—the gap that got more difficult every day for Christopher to ignore. The persona Dante adopted for TV—one he'd honed over the years, to make the network happy—bled into real life.

This time, that included the harsh and cruel attitude pointed at Julie, and that kind of clash with a business partner made everything worse. Christopher was tired of asking him to change the behavior. In less than two weeks, they'd shoot the special segment for Dante's show, featuring the kitschy bakery, and head back to L.A. That would be the end of most of the strain, one way or another. Dante's interaction with Julie would be limited to occasional meetings, and Andi would become his primary point of contact for investor and business information.

Dante scooted closer on the bed and

intertwined his fingers with Christopher's. "I'll try harder. I promise."

"Yeah. Okay." Something told Christopher that Dante and Julie were continents away from finding common ground. "The two of you should just fuck and get it over with." The taunt triggered something in his mind that he didn't intend—the desire to see Julie and Dante together. "Forget I said that."

"Would it help?" Dante asked.

"How could it possibly?"

"I know things are rocky between you and me." Dante sighed. "That you'd rather be home. You don't like how the show is going. I promise, when we make it through filming this segment, I'll talk to the studio about changes. Get your name up there with the associate-producer credits, where it belongs."

"It's not about Julie or having my name on the screen." So much for the fuzzy afterglow of sex.

"I understand that, but it's a stopgap." At least Dante realized the issue ran deeper.

Christopher wasn't sure if Dante specifically referred to screwing Julie or a general, random fling. Using sex as a way to break down walls was a holdover from Christopher's time as a therapist. He'd surrendered several of his practices when he quit the profession, but that one still made sense. Getting laid shifted the mind's perspective, and it was a pretty decent way to do so. "It could be. Bar this weekend?"

"Or ask Julie."

Christopher liked the suggestion. It didn't

matter how many ways he tried to talk himself out of it; he wouldn't mind if she was their playmate while they were here. "You can't stand her. That's what started this conversation."

"I don't have to like her, to watch you fuck her."

"You're not making this better." This contract couldn't end soon enough, as far as Christopher was concerned

The story continues in Chapter Two.

More by

Allyson Lindt

Roll Against Trust (3d20 Book 1)

The line between fantasy and reality blurs when a late night gaming session goes from playful to smoldering.

Tasha's not looking for love, but she doesn't mind just looking... and maybe a little fantasizing. Her two best friends and weekend AD& D buddies, Seth and Ryan, are the perfect guest stars in her fantasies. When a late night gaming session with the three goes from silly to verbally scorching in an instant, Tasha wonders if her imagination is enough to keep her satisfied long term.

Then her ex's money mismanagement catches up to her in the form of draining her bank account, her job is threatened by a mistake that points to Ryan, and Seth takes his side. If Tasha can't move past her trust issues long enough to uncover the truth—both with herself and the men she's falling for—she'll wind up broken-hearted and just plain broke.

The Nerds and the CEO

As long as Antonio has Justin and the Silicon Valley start-up they built together, Antonio's content to hide his true feelings. He'd rather keep Justin's friendship than confess his love and lose everything.

Justin's gotten careless with their business. He sees a different future for APPropriate Designs than their board of directors, and his drive to prove his way is right threatens the company's investment potential.

The board sends in their own contract developer to ensure their rules are being followed. Justin doesn't expect her to be the one-night-stand with home he played out the scorching fantasy of sharing her with Antonio.

Emily is drawn to both men, and as long hours and tight deadlines push them closer together, they heat up keyboards and the sheets. If their private hookups become public knowledge, she'll lose her job, they'll lose their company, and the three will be torn apart before they discover if all of them can find happily-ever-after with each other.

About the Author

Allyson Lindt is a full-time geek and a fuller-time contemporary romance author. She likes her stories with sweet geekiness and heavy spice, because cubicle dwellers need love too. She loves a sexy happily-ever-after and helping deserving cubicle dwellers find their futures together

Made in the USA
Middletown, DE
12 April 2019